"Reece," she said softly, "I'm not interested in a...relationship. It's not that—"

"Well, that's a good thing." He cut her off. "'Cause a relationship is the farthest thing from my mind."

Maggie's gaze darted to his face, a frown biting deeply into her brow. Confusion inundated her mind as she wondered how she should feel about his statement, how she should respond.

Then he chuckled.

The warm, silky rumble soothed away her frown, but she was still totally bewildered about exactly where this conversation was leading.

She heard the sensuous grin in his voice as he said, "I don't know if you've noticed, but I'm hot for you, Maggie."

She stifled a gasp. "Look, Reece," she began slowly, her voice sounding rusty. "Since neither one of us is looking to get involved, maybe we should try to...ah...to...ignore what it is we're feeling."

"Why on earth would we want to do that?"

Dear Reader,

Love is always in the air at Silhouette Romance. But this month, it might take a while for the characters of May's stunning lineup to figure that out! Here's what some of them have to say:

"I've just found out the birth mother of my son is back in town. What's a protective single dad to do?"—FABULOUS FATHER Jared O'Neal in Anne Peters's *My Baby, Your Son*

"What was I thinking, inviting a perfect—albeit beautiful—stranger to stay at my house?"—member of THE SINGLE DADDY CLUB, Reece Newton, from *Beauty and the Bachelor Dad* by Donna Clayton

"I've got one last chance to keep my ranch but it means agreeing to marry a man I hardly know!"—Rose Murdock from *The Rancher's Bride* by Stella Bagwell, part of her TWINS ON THE DOORSTEP miniseries

"Would you believe my little white lie of a fiancé just showed up—and he's better than I ever imagined!" —Ellen Rhoades, one of our SURPRISE BRIDES in Myrna Mackenzie's *The Secret Groom*

"I will not allow my search for a bride to be waylaid by that attractive, but totally unsuitable, redhead again!"—sexy rancher Rafe McMasters in *Cowboy Seeks Perfect Wife* by Linda Lewis

"We know Sabrina would be the perfect mom for us—we just have to convince Dad to marry her!"—the precocious twins from Gayle Kaye's *Daddyhood*

Happy Reading!

Melissa Senate
Senior Editor

Please address questions and book requests to:
Silhouette Reader Service
U.S.: 3010 Walden Ave., P.O. Box 1325, Buffalo, NY 14269
Canadian: P.O. Box 609, Fort Erie, Ont. L2A 5X3

BEAUTY AND THE BACHELOR DAD

Donna Clayton

Silhouette

R O M A N C E™

Published by Silhouette Books

America's Publisher of Contemporary Romance

For Melissa Jeglinski with lots of love and
appreciation—you are one extraordinary editor!

Many thanks to Donald C. Hash, Lt., Maryland State
Police, retired, for his technical assistance.

 SILHOUETTE BOOKS

ISBN 0-373-19223-1

BEAUTY AND THE BACHELOR DAD

Copyright © 1997 by Donna Fasano

Books by Donna Clayton

Silhouette Romance

Mountain Laurel #720
Taking Love in Stride #781
Return of the Runaway Bride #999
Wife for a While #1039
Nanny and the Professor #1066
Fortune's Bride #1118
Daddy Down the Aisle #1162
*Miss Maxwell Becomes a Mom #1211
*Nanny in the Nick of Time #1217
*Beauty and the Bachelor Dad #1223

*The Single Daddy Club

DONNA CLAYTON

is proud to be a recipient of the Holt Medallion, an award honoring outstanding literary talent. And seeing her work appear on the Waldenbooks Series Bestsellers List has given her a great deal of joy and satisfaction.

Reading is one of Donna's favorite ways to wile away a rainy afternoon. She loves to hike, too. Another hobby added to her list of fun things to do is traveling. She fell in love with Europe during her first trip abroad recently and plans to return often. Oh, and Donna still collects cookbooks, but as her writing career grows, she finds herself using them less and less.

The Single
Daddy Club

THE SINGLE DADDY CLUB
DECLARATION

We, the undersigned, do solemnly swear
to uphold the standards of the
Single Daddy Club. We shall be loving,
nurturing parents—proud of our single
status. Although female companionship
would be nice, we shall never be convinced
to enter into the state of matrimony solely
for the sake of our children.
(We shall, however, be happy to settle
down with the woman of our dreams...
if she ever shows up!)

Fatherhood forever!

Derrick Cheney Married

Jason Devlin Married *Russ Newton*
Soon to Wed?

Chapter One

"Are you the man in charge around here?"

Reece looked up from the photo he'd been staring at and focused his gaze on the woman who had poked her head into his office.

"Well...yes," he said, feeling a little taken aback by her sudden appearance. He hadn't heard her knock, and wondered if he could have been that engrossed in his thoughts. "I am."

He had no appointments scheduled this morning; however, he found himself glancing unwittingly at his calendar. Then the door opened wider and Joey, Reece's newest employee, stepped into the room.

"I told her she couldn't barge in on you like this." Joey's tone was even, but there was evidence of suppressed frustration. "I told her she needed an appointment. That you were too busy—"

"I am sorry," the woman said to Reece. "I don't mean to cause any trouble. But I couldn't seem to make him—" she indicated Joey with a nod of her head "—understand the scope of my…problem.'' Her frustration was not as well disguised as Joey's had been.

A distraction was just what he needed, Reece decided. Realizing that he still held the framed snapshot of his son in his hand, Reece pushed aside his parental worries and placed the picture on his desktop.

"Come in," he told the woman, standing up and automatically reaching to button his suit jacket.

She skirted around a frowning Joey.

Reece had spent most of the morning so preoccupied with thoughts of his son that he hadn't processed any of the claims that were stacked on his desk. However, he quickly understood as he looked at this woman, if it was a diversion he was looking for, this one was going to be a distraction and a half.

Her deep emerald eyes glittered with pique. Her height made her look formidable—five foot eight or nine, he guessed. The clothing she wore was formfitting: her knit top hugged softly rounded breasts, her tapered trousers— the kind with those little straps at the bottom—doing the same to the curves below her waist. But what Reece found most striking about the woman was her flaming red hair, its short and sassy cut silently shouting out the word *sexy*.

"Reece…"

The sound of Joey's voice drew his attention. For one quick and unsettling moment, Reece realized that his concentrated appraisal of the woman's physical beauty had made him forget that anyone else was in the room. He frowned. It had been a very long time since a female— any female—had averted his attention from his work to this degree. Instinctively, he cloaked his mind with apathy as if it were a suit of protective armor.

"I handled her insurance claim perfectly," the young man said firmly. "By the book. It's the *Dunlap* case."

The emphasis that Joey placed on the woman's last name wasn't lost on Reece.

He nodded. "I see," he said, remembering Joey's e-mail message regarding the woman's claim.

Suspected insurance fraud. The words rang in Reece's head. Well, she might be a beautiful woman, but he'd be damned if he'd allow her to rob his company.

Reece rounded his desk and reached for the file in Joey's hand. "I'm certain everything is in order," he told him. "However, maybe I can help Ms. Dunlap understand our...position."

The expression on Joey's face was full of silent argument. Reece raised his brows. Finally, the young man handed over the file and exited the office, closing the door behind him.

"Well, Ms. Dunlap," Reece said when they were alone, "how about if we talk?"

"I'd like that," she said. "And I'd like it, also, if you called me Maggie."

"Have a seat, Maggie," he said, walking back around his desk. "I'm Reece. Reece Newton. And I can see that your morning isn't going very well."

"That's an understatement," the woman murmured.

Her shapely behind whispered across the padded seat of the chair as she slid back, the sound of the gentle friction seeming to weaken the armor he'd donned. He swallowed hard, narrowing his eyes on the file that he flipped open on his desktop. Focus, darn it, he told himself.

"Is that your son?" she asked, casually pointing to the picture he'd been studying before she'd interrupted his day.

"Yes," Reece told her. He smiled at the boy's impish grin. "Jeff will be going to camp for two weeks. It'll be his first time away from home."

She nodded. "I'll bet you and your wife will miss him."

"It's just me and Jeff," Reece said, steeling himself for the surprise that always resulted when he told people that he was raising his son on his own. He could see the silent questions spark in Maggie Dunlap's eyes.

A father on his own with a child wasn't such a big deal these days. Two of his close friends had been, until just recently, in the same situation. Both of his buddies had women in their lives now, but that was something that would never happen to Reece. Not in a million years. He didn't need the anguish. Or the trouble.

And he didn't owe the woman who sat in his office any explanations or answers to her unspoken questions, either.

"If you'll give me a moment to familiarize myself with your claim…"

She nodded, and they both remained silent as Reece scanned the documents in front of him. Every time he blinked, Joey's suspicions flashed through his mind like bold-faced capital letters typed on a blank computer screen. *Suspected insurance fraud.*

Reece knew from years of experience that if the legitimacy of a claim was in question, it was best to induce the policy holder to talk as much as possible. Retelling the story often lent the claimant enough rope with which to hang himself, or rather, *herself* in this particular case.

He gazed at Maggie Dunlap, and couldn't help but marvel once again at how utterly gorgeous the woman was. Her almond-shaped eyes gave her creamy-skinned, hollow-cheeked face an exotic quality that was quite stunning.

Damn it, man, his mind silently railed. This woman just might be trying to steal your company blind.

And wasn't it just like a woman to do something like

this? Get something for nothing? And the beautiful ones were the worst.

Reece acknowledged that it was this kind of thinking that probably kept him in the fine state of living single, free of the entanglements of an intimate relationship. And it was exactly this kind of thinking he needed right now.

Granted, just as many men committed insurance fraud as did women. But that fact was so easy to ignore when his protective armor was in such desperate need of reinforcement. If apathy wasn't working, maybe he needed something a little stronger.

Leaning forward to rest his elbows on the desktop, Reece said, "Why don't you tell me what's been happening."

Maggie Dunlap's irritation over her circumstances was evident in her tight body posture.

"It's simple, really," she began. "I don't know why that guy—what was his name, Joey?—couldn't understand. My house was broken into last Tuesday. One of my video cameras was destroyed. I called the police. They issued a report. I contacted my insurance office. They sent Joey to assess the damage. And he's been giving me a hard time ever since. To tell you the truth, the man's been downright rude."

"I hope you'll allow me to apologize for Joey," Reece said. "His sister-in-law is in the hospital. She's in a coma. An accident of some kind. So Joey's under some stress with the worry of it."

Even as Reece offered the explanation, he was assessing Maggie Dunlap and her side of the situation. She had certainly sounded honest enough. Her story was short and to the point. And the fact that she'd looked him, unwaveringly, in the eye as she'd stated her case was very telling. Maggie Dunlap was either the best actress on the East

Coast, or she was telling the truth. Reece hoped like hell that his hormones weren't sabotaging his intuition.

"I'm sorry Joey's having a bad time," she said. Then she tilted her head a fraction to one side. "Are you going to be able to help me? Do you have the authority to put my claim through and issue me some money? Look, Mr. Newton—"

"Reece," he asserted. "Please, call me Reece." He gave his best professional smile. "I like to think this is a friendly office. And our first priority is making the customer happy. Since you feel that Joey has treated you rudely, I'd like to make every effort to make sure you're satisfied."

It wasn't until after he'd said the final word that he realized it could be taken as some sort of sexual double entendre. Thankfully, she didn't seem to notice.

"All I want is what I'm due." She tugged at a small curl of hair located at the back of her ear. "Is that too much to ask? I've paid monthly installments on an insurance policy which *supposedly* covered my video camera. The camera was destroyed, through no fault of my own. Your insurance company needs to pay up."

"Well, under normal circumstances, I'd agree with you wholeheartedly."

She straightened her spine. "Are you saying what happened to me wasn't a *normal* circumstance? What constitutes normal?" Then she added, "*If* you don't mind my asking."

He fought the grin that tugged at one corner of his mouth. This woman was full of spit and vinegar, and Reece was totally floored by how appealing he found her sassy attitude.

Again, he sternly reminded himself of Joey's dark and

dubious allegation against her. His smile dissolved in an instant.

"I guess, when a true crime is committed, there *is* no normal." He hesitated. "But maybe you could explain something to me," he went on quietly. "Help me to understand why the police report states that there was no sign of forced entry. Usually, when a house is broken into there is evidence left behind. Bent window frames from a pry bar of some kind, broken glass in a door that's been forced open."

The woman remained silent.

"And why do you think," he went on evenly, "that your seven-year-old video camera was the only item that was damaged? Why wasn't anything taken? Your TV, stereo, jewelry. That *is* the usual reason that someone breaks into a house—to take, to steal. To come away with something of value."

Her full, wine-colored lips tightened.

Finally, she simply whispered, "I don't know." Then her words increased in volume and in strength as she continued, "I don't have answers to any of your questions. Just as I didn't have answers for the police officer when *he* asked them. All I know is that my camera is worthless. Destroyed by a small, isolated fire. A fire that was not set by me. I need your company to pay me the money I'm due so I can purchase a new one. I have a business to run."

He forced himself to smile, but he made certain he kept it neutral. "And what kind of business do you run, Maggie?"

It was an irrelevant question. He knew very well that the information was surely somewhere in the woman's file. But he couldn't keep himself from asking. The sound of her voice was like heated satin flowing all around him, and even though he wanted to damn the very notion, he had to admit he wanted to hear more of it.

"I'm a private investigator."

Leave it to an extraordinary-looking woman to have an extraordinary occupation. He should have known she wouldn't have chosen a job as mundane as, say, a bank teller or a waitress or a corporate executive. As he contemplated it all, his brain became hazy around the edges and his curiosity got the best of him. His tone softened as he found himself asking, "And what sort of mysteries do you solve?"

Maggie's jewel green eyes studied him. Finally, she quietly said, "I take exception to being patronized, Mr. Newton."

Now he'd insulted the woman, and he hadn't even meant to ask the damned question. Hell, man, his analytical brain raged at him, get your hormones in check. You have a job to do. Quit thinking with your nether regions, and do it already!

"I certainly meant no offense."

Again, he felt scrutinized by her cool gaze. It was almost as though she was trying to figure out if he really wanted to know more about her job, or if he was being condescending.

She moistened her full bottom lip. "I don't mind telling you what I do for a living." Her chin dipped as she looked away from him for a moment. "I investigate—" her eyes returned to his "—wayward husbands."

When she didn't elaborate right away, Reece's brow creased as he wondered exactly what she meant by the odd description.

"Some of my clients call it 'fooling around,' or 'hanky-panky.' One woman told me her husband was 'getting some sugar on the side.' Adultery. Infidelity. Or good old fornication.'' She shrugged. ''Any of those terms will do.'' Her chest rose as she took a deep breath. ''The women who hire me might use different words to voice their suspicions, but there's always one thing they all have in common. They're desperate to know the truth. And I provide them with just that.''

There was something in the tilt of her head, something in the set of her jaw, that made Reece uncomfortable...almost as though he should feel responsible for every single low-life man she'd ever been paid to investigate. He shifted in his seat, sorry that he'd allowed his curiosity to break loose and ask the question to begin with.

''What do you say we focus on your problem,'' he told her. ''Let's get this claim processed.''

''Now you're talking,'' Maggie said.

She scooted to the edge of her seat, and Reece kept his eyes riveted to the papers, desperately pushing from his mind the sexy image of her trouser-clad bottom inching forward in the chair.

Remember, this woman just might be trying to rook the company, he told himself. She was like every other woman he'd ever met in his life—hiding something, deceiving someone or looking out for her own best interests. He needed to keep that thought to the forefront of his mind.

He looked up from the forms. ''I have to tell you,'' he began quietly, ''that I tend to agree with Joey's conclusion that this claim should be denied.''

He darted a glance at Maggie and saw her perfectly arched brows draw into a frown. ''Give me a second to explain.'' He eased back in his chair. ''Let's look, just for a moment, at the fact that, if someone broke into your home—''

"If?"

Maggie Dunlap's shoulders squared, making it completely obvious that she took exception to his choice of words.

"Okay," he relented. "One is left to surmise that whoever broke into your home, did so with little or no trouble. You can't hold my company liable for your home, or your possessions, if you don't keep your doors and windows locked. Could it be possible, Maggie, that you left your home—?"

"No, it is not possible," she cut him off. "I lock my doors. And my windows. I'm not an idiot."

"I'm not insinuating that you are," he said. "For the sake of argument, let's say you make a habit of locking your doors and windows. Let's say someone *did* break into your home. Let's say someone *did* destroy your video camera."

Her luscious mouth pursed just enough so that her full bottom lip rounded just a bit. The resulting pouty pucker was nearly Reece's undoing.

Keeping his gaze fastened securely to hers, he continued, "Let's talk about the damage that was done versus the amount of money you're looking to claim."

"The camera is worthless," she pointed out.

"I'm sure it is." He hesitated a moment, wanting to make an impression with his next question. "Tell me, Maggie, how much do you think your seven-year-old video camera was worth...*before* it had been damaged?"

Direct hit! Maggie Dunlap's green-eyed gaze averted for a moment. She shifted in her seat, propped an elbow on the chair's armrest, then eased it back down to her side.

When she didn't answer for some seconds, he rephrased

the question. "Do you really believe technology that dated is worth...anything?"

She looked at him then, her eyes narrowing to a glare. "Granted," she said, "I bought the camera secondhand. But the darned thing has to be worth something. Why else would I have paid to have it insured?"

"Placing monetary value on your personal possessions isn't my company's responsibility. That is, until you want us to pay for them or replace them."

Her mouth thinned. Finally, she said, "So. You're not going to give me anything?"

He thought it best to stifle his urge to shrug. "The camera wasn't worth anything, Maggie."

She tilted up her chin, her jaw jutting forward aggressively. "I have a good mind to call the state insurance commissioner. I'm sure he'd like to hear about this... this..."

Reece's eyebrows and his ire rose at her challenge. "And I may have to put a call into his office myself. You might like to know that he has an entire staff of people eager to go after criminals who are trying to defraud insurance companies."

The chair Maggie Dunlap was sitting in scooted backward several inches when she stood with force. "I am *not* trying to defraud anyone! There was a tape in that camera when it was destroyed. A tape that contained proof that took me weeks to get. A tape that would have been worth money from a client. I know you and...and Joey out there both think I burned up my own camera so I could update my equipment with money from your insurance company. But it simply doesn't make sense that I would destroy evidence that has cost me time and income."

A tense silence hovered between them.

"I didn't know about the tape." Reece sat back in his

chair. "That information's not in the police report. And if what you're telling me is true, then you're right, it doesn't make sense." He felt more confused than ever about Joey's suspicions regarding this woman.

"Look, Maggie," he said, "I'm not only the senior claims adjuster in this office—I also act as the insurance investigator for southern Maryland. I can look into this for you. It will take me a week or so to get out from under all these files." He placed the palm of his hand on top of the pile of manila files that sat on his desk.

Her body visibly relaxed. "I'd appreciate your help," she said at last. "I know you're going to find that I'm telling the truth...so is there any way you could give me just enough money to buy myself another camera?"

Reece felt badly, but he shook his head. "My hands are tied, Maggie. I can't." He looked down at the file. "And an investigation—no matter what the findings— won't change the fact that the camera was overinsured."

The woman inhaled deeply. At last, she said, "I guess there's nothing left to say."

She stood there, defeat evident in every stiff muscle of her body. For some godforsaken reason—one that Reece couldn't fathom at the moment—he was besieged by the oddest desire to somehow fix this for her. To do something that would make her day a little less miserable.

Unable to understand why, he found himself saying, "Look, Maggie, I feel terrible about this. I really do. Let me contact your insurance agent. I'm sure I can get him to refund to you the portion of your premium that's been going toward insuring that outdated camera. It won't be much, but it'll be more than what you have now, which is nothing."

Her jaw muscles clenched tight, honing her hollow-cheeked face into sharper, sexier angles. And just when he thought she was going to turn him down, she nodded her head slowly and said, "I'll take it."

Maggie Dunlap turned on her heel, pulled open the door and marched out of his office. And from his excellent vantage point, he was able to watch her subtly swaying fanny as she walked the entire length of the hall.

The sharp, rumbling *pug-pug-pug-pug* of the motorcycle engine jerked Maggie to attention. Her heart pounded furiously, and she rushed to the window to peek through the drawn shades. But all she saw was the red brake light of the bike as it slowed to turn the corner and disappear.

Maggie stared out the window and waited, every muscle tense, ready.

Finally, she exhaled.

"I hate this!" She flung herself away from the window. "I hate feeling afraid." And for the moment, her fear was displaced by an all-consuming anger.

She'd never experienced this kind of panicky apprehension before—a mind-numbing anxiety that had her looking over her shoulder every few moments.

Under normal circumstances, she'd always thought of herself as a pretty courageous person. One would have to be in order to work in her profession. She'd faced many angry men—husbands of her clients who were mighty upset to have been caught, via a photograph or videotape, in one compromising position or another. Yes, normally she was anything but fearful.

But someone had been invading her home. Someone had been violating the sanctity of her very own private space. On a daily basis.

Oh, she had no concrete evidence. That was the most frustrating thing about it.

The episodes had begun over a week ago with the

senseless destruction of her video camera. She hadn't recognized the act as the beginning of anything, had only thought it was an isolated case of miscreant teens out for an evening of malicious mischief.

Maggie had been baffled, and irritated, by the fact that the perpetrators had left behind no sign of having forced their way into her house. She'd had no answers for the police when they had questioned her about the lack of evidence. In fact, she remembered explaining it away, using the phrase, "the more criminally wizened youth of today." Maggie hadn't even tried to explain her thoughts to the rude insurance adjuster, Joey something-or-other. Or his boss—the handsome, yet no help whatsoever, Reece Newton.

Funny how she still remembered the man's name so clearly. With her carefully fostered bad attitude regarding the male of the species, actual names usually melted from her brain like ice chips on a sun-heated sidewalk. But Reece Newton...

His name *and* image had remained firmly planted in her mind for days and days. His thick, dark hair, those smoky, dark eyes, his strong, handsome face...those had been the memories she'd focused on to dispel her night terrors—

"Enough already!" she scolded herself, and she refocused her thoughts on the problem at hand—the first of many intrusive visits into her home by person or persons unknown.

The police had explained to her that the fire that had destroyed her camera had been controlled. Which meant that whoever had set it had stayed around to see that the flames hadn't grown and consumed her entire house. That had only cemented in her mind the idea of miscreant teens—out to do damage, but not too much damage. However, the police hadn't agreed with her scenario at all. Instead, the two officers had cast suspicious glances at her the entire time they were in her house. It was no wonder the insurance company had refused her claim, after the report the police officers had supplied that pointed invisible fingers of guilt directly at her.

It had taken her nearly a week to finally admit the other weird things taking place under her roof. They were small things: her favorite teacup moved from one side of the cabinet to the other, throw pillows bunched at one side of the couch when she knew she always placed one at each end, her shower door left open when she made a habit of keeping it closed.

Small, eerie things. Things that had her second-guessing herself. Had she really left the magazines a mess on the coffee table? She *knew* she hadn't.

And then the incidents got a little more frequent, their scope a little larger: a sprinkling of instant-coffee crystals dotting the kitchen counter when she never drank coffee, the back door left wide open when she was absolutely certain she'd locked up the house before leaving.

The open door had really given her the creeps. Actually, it had put the fear of God into her. She'd had dead bolts installed, and she'd begun sleeping with her .380 pistol nearby instead of locked in the desk drawer where she usually kept it. She'd begun jumping at noises. Paranoia had slowly seeped into her bones, and little by little, her self-confidence in keeping herself safe had trickled away like water from a leaky barrel.

Who the hell was playing this game with her? And why?

She glanced over at the files scattered across her dining-room table. It had to be one of the men she was currently investigating. One of her clients' husbands was warning her off. Threatening her. There was no doubt in her mind whatsoever now—not after the mess she'd found in her garage this morning.

Her head snapped up at the sound of a car cruising slowly past the front of her house. She was at the window in a flash. In the dusky light of late afternoon, she watched the car slow to a crawl, and then come to a complete stop.

Adrenaline shot through her body like hot acid. She ran toward the back of the house, jerked open the drawer of the nightstand and extracted her gun. Its smooth, stainless-steel handle fit in her palm with a cool and accustomed comfort.

The hours and hours she spent at the practice range every month gave her the skill and confidence to handle the gun. And she was leaning heavily on her ten years of law-enforcement experience—experience that was a requirement for her private-investigator's license—for the knowledge and judgment she would need if she ever felt the necessity to pull the trigger.

Maggie had never shot anyone. Had never felt threatened enough to actually protect herself with the gun she'd owned for years. But she did feel threatened enough now.

And she wouldn't be taken unawares. Not ever again.

Chapter Two

Reece searched in the dwindling light for a house number, and when he finally found it, he turned the car into the driveway and cut the engine. The small Cape Cod was dark, the curtains pulled. His secretary had assured him that Maggie Dunlap would be expecting him. Reece hoped he hadn't driven halfway to Salisbury for nothing.

Reece's secretary had alerted him this morning—the infamous Maggie was making another claim, this one against her auto insurance. Apparently, something had happened to completely disable her car. Maggie had bypassed Joey altogether, instead calling Reece's secretary.

Thoughts of the fiery redhead had plagued him all week long, and even though he would die before admitting it out loud, he'd worked hard to clear his desk so that he could conduct the investigation he'd promised her. Worry and uncertainty gnawed at his gut like an irritating little mouse. He found out, via his secretary, that Maggie had sounded stressed, nearly frantic, when she'd called. Had her home and property been once again vandalized? he wondered. Or was this just another great "acting job" on Maggie's part? Answering those questions, Reece guessed, was going to be his hardest task.

As he looked at the darkened house, he only hoped she was home.

Of course, her car could be in the garage; however, vandals usually attacked automobiles that were within easy access—parked out on the street or on the driveway. And as Maggie's car had been supposedly totally impaired...

He pressed his lips together in a thin line as he gathered his things together. Wouldn't it be ironic if she were to drive up in a car that she'd claimed had been disabled by hooligan teenagers? He'd had things like that happen in the past. Yet again, her claim could be quite legitimate. Her car could very well have been wrecked during the night by a roving band of rowdy juvenile delinquents.

Before heading toward the house, Reece made sure he had his trusty Polaroid camera. Documentation was everything in his line of business.

No sooner had he rung the bell than the door swung open.

Reece stood there, having to actually study the woman a moment to be sure she was the same Maggie Dunlap who had been in his office just last week. The velvety peach skin he remembered was now milky pale, her green gaze hauntingly suspicious. She darted a quick glance over his shoulder, toward his car, then to the opposite side of the property before she looked at his face again. The dark smudges under her eyes made him frown.

"Uh..." he said when she didn't greet him, "you were expecting me?"

"Yes."

She nodded, and he couldn't help but notice how jerky and unnatural the movement seemed.

Then she gave a tired sigh. "Well, I did forget, but…"

Maggie hesitated, as if she'd just remembered something important.

"Wait there just a minute," she told him.

Through the screen door, Reece watched as she went to the small desk that sat against the far wall of the small living room. Her back was to him, but it looked as if she opened the topmost drawer, placed something inside and then closed it. Immediately, she turned and came back to the door.

"Come in," she said, pushing wide the screen. "I'm glad you're here to look at my car."

Reece moved into the living room, but the fact that she took a second to scan the front lawn before closing the front door didn't escape him.

"Are you okay?" he asked.

"I'm fine."

Her gaze narrowed the slightest bit—something he took as a silent challenge. It was clear she didn't want him asking questions. Well, he really didn't care what she wanted. Her behavior made doubts arise in his mind. He wasn't going to forget about them simply because she didn't feel up to being quizzed.

He shrugged. "You just seem a little…edgy."

"Everything's great."

But the expression she forced into her tone let him know everything was anything but great.

"Everything's fine. Let's go look at the car."

She went past him, and he followed.

"It's in the garage," she said as she passed through the kitchen.

They went into a small laundry room, and Reece was

impressed by how orderly and neat the house was. And when she opened the door that led to the garage, the tidy condition of the area told him that Maggie Dunlap was a highly organized person. Just like himself. His own garage was meticulously kept. A place for every tool, and every tool in its place. He kept his home the same way. It was a quirk for which he took a great deal of good-natured harassment from his friends, Jason and Derrick.

He silently followed Maggie around to the far side of the car, and just as he was about to ask her to explain the problem, he saw it.

The pile of sand that sat on the floor of the garage was fairly large. A set of keys dangled from the lock on the open gas cap.

"This happened *inside* the garage?" Reece couldn't keep the surprise from his voice. "And I see that whoever did this got hold of your keys."

Maggie only nodded, her lips pressed together tightly as her face paled further.

"Did you leave the garage open last night?"

"No." Her tone was a mere whisper.

A frown of bewilderment bit deeply into his brow.

"I don't understand how this happened," he said. "What did the police have to say?"

The silence that filled the room made him feel uneasy.

"Maggie?" He stood stock still. "You *did* call the police, right?"

Her gaze veered toward the floor. Reece watched as her tongue darted out to smooth across her lips, and then the muscles in her long, elegant neck tensed as she swallowed.

"Maggie?" The sharpness in his tone contained enough force to draw her emerald eyes upon his face once more.

"Why?" he asked, the tiny word sounding incredulous and husky even to his own ears. "Why would you not call the police?"

She studied him, and it seemed as though a thousand thoughts were flying through her head.

Finally, her chin lifted a fraction. "Look, I just don't have any answers for you."

She seemed to become more agitated, more upset with each word she spoke.

"Please..."

Reece saw her chin becoming trembly with emotion. The sight made his mouth go dry.

"Just take your pictures and...fill out your paperwork. Just do your job and leave me alone!"

She turned and stormed out of the garage and into the house.

The sand on the concrete floor ground underfoot as he stepped toward the car. What the hell was going on here? he wondered. Who would want to do such a thing to her car? Sand dumped in the gas tank was a malicious prank that kids usually played on people they disliked. What could the woman have done to evoke this kind of behavior from someone?

Another thought occurred to him—could she have done it herself? She was already suspected of destroying her own videotape recorder. Why not go for a new car, too?

The idea just didn't ring true, he decided. Maybe he could think such a thing if the car were older. But noting the make and model, he realized that the car had been purchased just last year. Maggie was most certainly still making payments on it. And she just didn't strike him as being stupid enough to try to pull a stunt like this. She would have at least moved the car outside.

Besides, there was something different about Maggie

Dunlap. She was edgy. But it wasn't the kind of edginess that was brought on by a guilty conscience. He'd seen that in people often enough to recognize it. No, Maggie was acting jumpy. Nervous.

Afraid.

As the word floated into his brain, Reece absently bent over and set his briefcase onto the floor. He looked once again at the pile of sand at his feet, rubbing his fingers back and forth across his jaw in worried contemplation.

"I think I have everything I need." Reece came into the kitchen, and Maggie looked up at him from where she sat at the oval-shaped oak table.

"However," he went on, "I do have a few questions that need answering."

Her fingers tensed around the mug she held. "Somehow, I was certain you would." The sigh she heaved sounded weary. "Sit down. Can I offer you something to drink? Tea? Or would you rather have something cold…a soda?"

"No, I'm fine, thank you." He pulled out a chair and sat down directly across from her. There were several sections on the claim form that needed filling out, but those could wait.

The questions he wanted to ask, the concern he wanted to impart, had nothing to do with car insurance or claim forms. Maggie Dunlap was in some kind of trouble, and he had an overwhelming urge to reach out to her.

Bending forward just a little, Reece rested his elbows on the tabletop. "Maggie—"

"Don't."

Her gaze pierced him like tiny, razor-sharp needles, and the sheer force of negativity pouring from her caused him to sit back in the chair.

"Let's keep this simple," she told him quietly, "and professional. Don't ask me any questions of a personal nature."

Okay, Reece, he told himself. She's made it abundantly clear she's not interested in your concern. He couldn't help feeling insulted by her rejection. He was embarrassed, too. It was almost as if he'd reached his hand out to the woman, and she'd slapped it aside.

And just like any other red-blooded male, he did what came naturally—he got angry. Oh, it wasn't the kind of fury that flared up and made a man say things he didn't mean. It was more a slow-burning irritation that simmered just below the surface.

"Simple and professional," he said, keeping his tone as even as he could. "I think I can handle that."

The kitchen was quiet a moment, then she said, "I was certain you could."

But could he?

There were...things...strange electric sparks that swirled all around them. The very air was heavy with unmentioned strain. Ineffable emotion snapped and flashed like lightning bolts, crashed like thunder. Was he sensing the edginess and fear emanating from Maggie? Or was it something else, something between the two of them that churned up the atmosphere?

To sit here and ignore this...this invisible storm seemed ludicrous to Reece. However, he would. Because Maggie Dunlap had demanded it.

He set his briefcase on its side, snapped open the brass latches and lifted the top. The paperwork he needed was right at hand, and he pulled the folder out, setting it in front of him on the table.

"This damage to your car," he began, "*is* covered.

Vandalism, fire and theft are covered one hundred percent...."

Her overwhelming relief at his words had her breath leaving her in an audible exhalation, and she sank against the back of the chair.

"Thank God," she whispered.

"However..."

His grave tone was like a powerful magnet that attracted her gaze to his in a flash. She became utterly still, every muscle in her body tensed as she waited for him to go on.

"Without a police report, you can't expect my company to file this claim as vandalism."

She didn't speak for a moment. Her eyes dipped down toward the ceramic mug. And when she looked at him, her gaze was shadowed with the same fear he'd noticed before.

"You know I didn't do that to my own car."

He nodded slowly, and then he sighed. "I don't mean to be the bad guy here. I'm only trying to do my job."

Again, she studied him. The unseen, unheard bolts of energy tightened and burst and recoiled in the air. And yet again, he felt a tremendous urge to get involved in this lady's troubles, to ask her what was going on in her life, to offer some sort of help, or solace, or advice.

Damn it! he silently railed at himself. Hasn't she made it perfectly clear she isn't interested in your help? Hell, this was a *woman* sitting here in front of him. A *woman!* he reminded himself. And he'd never met a woman yet who wasn't secretive, and conniving, and out for just what she could get for herself.

"So, where does that leave me?"

The heated velvet of her voice wrapped him in a balmy blanket, soothing the cursing and spitting viciousness in him. Immediately, he felt chagrined, almost embarrassed by the fact that he'd allowed his thoughts to veer so far off track.

Simple and professional. He repeated the words several times in his head. He could do this. He could look at Maggie Dunlap and see her—not as a beautiful woman in obvious trouble—but as a policy holder in need of his services as an employee of her insurance company. He *would* do it!

"Well," he began, "as I said before, the damage is covered. But without a police report, I'll have to place the claim under comprehensive. That means we'll tow the car, have the gas tank and gas line replaced...we'll even pay for a rental until your car is ready." He hesitated before delivering the bad news. "But you will be responsible for your deductible. And that amounts to the first five hundred dollars."

"The first five hundred dollars?" Her green eyes went wide. "I don't have the first *five* dollars, let alone the first five hundred."

Tapered fingertips smoothed gracefully back and forth across her forehead. "What the heck am I supposed to do?"

Her question was rhetorical, he knew. And he was just as certain that she wasn't even speaking to him.

"I mean—" her jewel green eyes were filled with worry when she looked at him "—I can live without my video camera if I have to," she said. "I'll take still shots with my 35 mm." Then she shook her head. "But I can't possibly do my job without my car. I simply—" her hands flung out "—can't."

An odd metallic sound interrupted them. Reece wasn't startled so much by the noise; however, Maggie's violent reaction to it had him completely baffled.

"What—?"

"Shh, shh," she commanded quietly, every muscle in her slim body tense, her eyes alert.

She reached up along the wall and flipped off the overhead light.

"Stay here," she whispered.

"But, Maggie—"

Her eyes widened in silent warning, cutting off further speech. She slipped from her chair without a sound and left him sitting in the gloomy light all alone.

"Crazy woman," he muttered as he got up and moved across the room to look out the small kitchen window.

The backyard was wooded and shrouded in dusky shadows. He craned his neck to look, first in one direction and then the other, but he wasn't able to see a thing. He went out through the laundry room to the back door, opened it and stepped out into the warm summer evening.

It was a nice yard. A little overgrown maybe, but the trees and full, unpruned bushes gave everything a wild and woodsy feel. He liked it.

Reece stopped short when he heard the scrabbling metallic sound again. His gaze traveled up along one corner of the house. He grinned at what he saw there.

"I told you to stay in the kitchen!"

Maggie's harsh whisper took him completely by surprise, and his smile faded.

"Get in here!"

Her tone was just a little louder this time, and as he saw her standing there at the screen door, there was something about the stiff set of her shoulders that made him frown. He obeyed her order.

As he got closer, he recognized the look in her eyes as sheer panic. Her face was a ghostly white, her facial muscles tense.

"It's okay," he told her.

"Get in! Get in now!"

He pulled open the door and stepped inside. "Maggie, what—?"

The sight of the pistol in her hand dissolved the rest of his words. He simply looked at her peering out at the yard, at some unseen...attacker...or intruder.

The idea that someone had made this woman so afraid that she'd rushed to grab a gun—a gun!—at the least noise enraged him. And the fact that he had wanted her to confide in him, he'd wanted to offer her some kind of help and she'd flat out refused him only made him want to vent his anger on her. It wasn't logical; he knew that for damned sure. But who the hell bothered with logic at a time like this?

"It's a damned squirrel," he said.

He took her by the upper arm, shoved open the screen door and pulled her into the backyard. She followed him on legs as rigid and unyielding as wooden sticks.

When he got far enough from the house to see the corner of the roof, he pointed.

"See?" His eyes darted to the bushy-tailed squirrel that sat frozen in place. "A damned squirrel! Hunting for a damned acorn in the damned gutter! What are you going to do, Maggie? Shoot it?"

The daylight was almost completely gone now, and Reece glared down into Maggie's gaunt, frozen features. She appeared to be in some kind of fear-induced trance that had each and every muscle and tendon stiff and ready to react.

Suddenly, her entire body began to tremble. Her gaze bounced from the corner of the house where the squirrel had just scampered away, to his face and then back to the corner of the house. When her chin quivered, she clamped her bottom lip between her teeth in an obvious effort to control herself. Still, the anger that filled him was enough to make him want to shake her.

However, her tears were his undoing. Fat tears moistened her eyes and rolled slowly down her pale cheeks, scalding the icy layer of anger that surrounded his heart, melting the irrational fury that had him snapping and snarling at her.

Couldn't he see that what she needed was just a little comforting?

No sooner had the question flitted through his mind than he was wrapping her in his arms.

"It's okay," he crooned. "It's going to be okay."

He wasn't surprised when she crumpled against his chest. Maybe he should have been, but he wasn't.

"It isn't okay." Her voiced cracked with a suppressed sob. "It isn't."

Reece felt her hands grip his back as she seemed to hold on for dear life.

"Someone was in my house, Reece," she said against his chest. "Someone was in my house while I was asleep."

He got Maggie into the house and seated once more at the kitchen table. Once the gun had been put away in the desk drawer, Reece flipped on the dim light directly over the table and then reheated Maggie's mug of tea in the microwave. All the while, she released her pent-up stress with a steady stream of gentle tears. When he placed the steaming mug in front of her, she had stopped crying, but she was trembling so that he had to force himself not to reach out and take her in his arms again. The woman was absolutely scared to death.

"There was a trail of sand—" her tone held a thin,

ghostly quality that made the hairs at the base of Reece's skull stand on end "—from the garage, through the kitchen and hall and up the stairs." Maggie stared off into one corner of the darkened room. "Whoever was inside left a nice little pile of sand right outside my bedroom door."

Reece breathed a curse under his breath as he absently slid into a chair across from her, a dozen questions flooding his brain.

"It was so...scary," she rambled on. "I mean, I knew someone had been coming in. From the little things that had been moved...tampered with. I think he wanted me to know. But it was always when I wasn't home. I never had a problem while I was here—"

"This wasn't the first time? You *knew* someone was breaking in?" His voice was sharp as the questions burst from him. "Who the hell would do such a thing? Why didn't you call the police?"

Her gaze rose to his face. "They already believe I'm a nutcase. The officers who were here about my video camera practically came right out and accused me of committing the dastardly deed." Her tone lowered as she added, "So did you."

"But..."

"I'm not going to call the police and be humiliated again." Her gaze averted to the dark recesses of the far end of the kitchen. "I can take care of myself."

There was uncertainty in her words, and the fear emanating from her made Reece feel agitated.

"You can't stay here," he blurted out. "It isn't safe. If someone's getting in without forcing a door or a window, then he must have keys. Did you change the locks?"

Maggie nodded. "And I was going to have it done

again this weekend...I'm due to be paid by a client on Friday.''

"Maggie, you can't stay here," he repeated. "Is there somewhere you can go? Your parents' house? A brother or sister? A friend? You need to get out of here until you can find out who's doing this." He sat up straighter. "And you have to call the police—''

"No. No police. Believe me, I have my reasons.''

She hadn't raised her voice, but the curtness with which she'd cut him off made him sit back and blink.

Her throat muscles tightened as she swallowed. "And I have no place to go." She tipped up her chin. "Besides, I won't be chased out of my own home.''

"But this place isn't safe.''

Wrapping her fingers around the mug, she squeezed it between her pale hands. "I told you, Reece. I have no-where to go.''

Reece's mind was running a mile a minute. Maggie had been living with this fear for days on end. It was a wonder she wasn't a raving lunatic by now. He felt an urge to help her somehow—an urge that was so overwhelming, it grew and expanded in his mind until it cut off all other thought.

"Then you'll come home with me." The words were out of his mouth before he even realized he'd spoken.

"What? No way," she said.

"You're not safe here.''

"And what makes you think I'll be safe with you?''

Their gazes met and locked, and the air in the room grew suddenly still and heavy. Something he wasn't quite able to discern seemed to reach out to envelop him utterly and completely.

Attraction.

What a god-awful time to feel such a thing. It was ridiculous! Almost laughable.

But he wasn't laughing.

And it wasn't because of any physical attraction he felt toward Maggie Dunlap that he was offering her refuge under his roof. The woman was in trouble. And she was afraid. So afraid that she was waving a pistol at innocent wildlife.

He inhaled deeply. "You want to spend another night in this house alone?"

Immediately, she tucked her bottom lip between her even white teeth and said nothing. Although she tried to hide it, fear shadowed her gaze.

He nodded. "Then it's settled."

Chapter Three

"Home, sweet home." Reece pushed open the front door and invited Maggie, with a sweep of his hand, to enter.

The overnight bag she carried held her makeup and toiletries. Her overstuffed briefcase contained every single file she ever kept on her current and past clients. Reece hefted the heavier tapestried canvas bag in which she'd hurriedly packed some clothing.

"Come on," he said. "I'll show you the guest room."

She watched him move past her to the stairs, and she followed him up. He was a big man—probably an inch or two over six feet tall, and his body looked as solid as the proverbial Rock of Gibraltar. From the back, his shoulders were broad, his waist trim. His tailored business suit accentuated his build, and Maggie found herself wondering if those trousers hugged his butt beneath the material of his jacket.

Maggie's eyes widened, the risqué thought making her cheeks suffuse with heat. She was grateful that Reece's back was to her and that he didn't witness her schoolgirl blush. The fact that her brain, which had been so filled with fear and chaos when Reece had arrived at her home, was in any shape to even notice his physique was all due to Reece himself.

She couldn't believe how he'd succeeded in calming her down during the ride to his home. He'd purposefully talked about mundane things. Maggie had smiled at his funny, often outrageous, experiences as an insurance investigator and the people who tried to dupe the company. He'd squeezed her heart when he'd spoken of his son and the loneliness he'd felt since Jeff had been away at camp. He'd told her about a club of sorts that he and two of his friends had created. Apparently, when they had started out, they had been a small group of single guys in need of support in parental practices and personal matters. He'd actually grimaced when he'd stated that the other two men now had women in their lives, but the tone of Reece's voice had proved that he cared deeply about his buddies. He'd gone on to give her his opinion regarding local politics, and just when she thought he couldn't possibly find anything else to converse about, he'd ended up commenting on the latest television-talk-show topics.

She hadn't been required to say one word during the entire drive. But that hadn't kept her thoughts from churning. She should have explained to him all her reasons for refusing to call the police. She should have told him about—

No, she cut off the thought. It would be foolish to tell anyone, especially when she didn't know who she could trust.

Was it fair to drag this man into her dangerous situation? The question had been haunting her. She'd had every intention of refusing his offer of sanctuary. But then, he'd asked her if she wanted to spend another night alone, and her fear had pushed aside all her good intentions.

Finally, she'd allowed herself to become lost in the sound of Reece's voice. She'd realized early on that he was striving for some sense of normalcy. Ordinary, everyday conversation that was meant to lull her into a more relaxed state. His ploy had worked, and Maggie had been grateful for his efforts.

"That's Jeff's room," he said as he passed the first bedroom. "There's the bathroom. The room at the end of the hallway—" he pointed "—is mine, and here's where you'll stay." He stopped just outside the door and tossed a wide grin at her.

However, it wasn't just an ordinary grin—it was an expression filled with so much charm and openhearted welcome that it stole her breath away.

She stopped, right there in the hallway. The air felt suddenly thick, and Maggie thought her heart would pound a hole right through her rib cage. It wasn't as if she'd never seen the man smile before; he'd been full of business friendliness and finesse the first time she'd met him in his office. But this was different.

The lines that bracketed his mouth seemed almost fresh, as if smiling was not something he did often. But what that smile, combined with honest emotion, did to his already handsome features! Lord, the man should gift the world with that grin twenty-four hours a day.

His eyes were a dark mahogany in the light thrown by the overhead fixture, and they glittered warmly. Maggie moistened her suddenly dry lips. Why did Reece Newton have to be so darned good-looking?

Good-looking, heck, her brain silently chimed in, the man was downright gorgeous!

She forced herself to step through the doorway into the room that would be hers for the time being.

"It's nice," she said. But she didn't really see the room at all. Her brain seemed to be on overload having to deal with that awesome smile. "Thank you—" her voice lowered an octave, and she poured into it every ounce of heartfelt emotion that surged through her "—for everything."

In that instant, she was struck with the revelation of exactly what this man was doing for her. He'd opened up his home to her—a virtual stranger—when she'd had no place else to go. He'd worked hard to make her feel calm and composed...and safe. Feeling overwhelmed with it all, she looked away.

A quivery giddiness had her stomach feeling jumpy as she looked at him through lowered lashes. "I'll try hard to stay out of your way. I don't want to be an inconvenience."

"Nonsense," he said, ushering her into the room and setting the canvas bag down on the floor.

His tone had grown hoarse, and even though he'd only spoken one small word, she could tell that the monumental emotion stirring inside her was affecting him, too. It was as if there was some kind of bond between them now that he'd reached out to her. A sudden awkwardness sprang up between them.

Maggie made a great fuss over placing her briefcase and overnight bag on the upholstered chair that sat in one corner of the room.

"The chest of drawers is empty," Reece said. "And there should be plenty of space in the closet. There're hangers in there, too. You'll find clean towels in the linen closet across from the bathroom."

He talked quickly, trying, Maggie knew, to regain that

same sense of normalcy he'd conjured on the drive from her house.

"I'll bring fresh sheets for the bed," he went on. "The mattress is firm. I hope you like lots of support."

Reece sat down and gave the edge of the mattress a little bounce, and she knew he was looking at her, waiting for her to offer a friendly, mundane response in return.

"I'm sure it'll be fine." But the words were strained at best. Maggie knew it, and she saw that Reece noticed it, too.

Her gaze darted to the bed, and then back up to his face. In the periphery of her vision, she saw him smooth his palm across the spread, and for some reason, that simple action seemed to change everything.

The awkwardness between them swirled and thickened and metamorphosed into something new, something strangely intimate. Whatever it was, it had Maggie feeling terribly aware of each second that passed, completely perceptive of each move of Reece's body, each breath she herself inhaled.

Obviously, he, too, was cognizant of this…this *thing*.

And that's exactly how Maggie had identified it—a living, breathing, feeling thing. What in the world was going on here?

Reece stood up and walked to the window. The suddenness of his brisk action was like an unexpected snapping of fingers that jerked her to attention. She blinked, and the *thing* seemed to dissolve into nothingness. The air cleared and was once again breathable.

"Let me get out of here," he told her. "You have some unpacking to do." He looked at his watch. "And I'm due to meet with my buddies. You know, the guys I told you about? I hope you don't mind if I go out for a while.…"

"Oh, of course not," she said, feeling that he couldn't

walk out that door fast enough to suit her, yet at the same time, she didn't ever want him to leave. It was such a curious and odd sensation. One that baffled the heck out of her.

With a quick smile and a nod, he was gone.

Maggie didn't move from her spot there by the chair. She stood listening to him descending the stairs, wondering if what she and Reece had experienced just a moment ago had all been conjured by her imagination.

The scary thing was, she knew imagination had absolutely nothing to do with it.

"So you rode in on your white horse..."

Derrick was laughing so hard he had to stop talking. Reece only glared at his friend.

"And scooped up the poor damsel in distress," Derrick was finally able to finish.

Jason couldn't hold back his snickers any longer, and he joined Derrick. "And carried her off to the castle."

"Yeah," Reece growled, "and I hope both of you jokers choke on your beer."

Derrick and Jason tried hard to force serious expressions onto their faces, then made the mistake of catching each other's eyes. Their uproarious laughter drew the attention of the other customers in the small sports pub.

"Look, I'm not in the mood, okay?" Reece tipped up the smoky-colored beer bottle and took a long swallow. He tried to focus on the ball game playing on the big-screen TV at the far corner of the room as he asked, "What was I supposed to do? The woman was scared."

The excuse sounded lame, even to him. He guessed he deserved the jeers and jokes his buddies were making about his behavior. But that didn't mean he had to like it. He saw both of them grinning like oafs.

"Hey," he said seriously, "I said I'm not in the—"

"Okay, okay," Jason said. He nudged Derrick, who was still having trouble getting his humor in check.

As if running interference for Derrick, to give the man a few more seconds to compose himself, Jason went on, "It's just that we never expected something like this from you, Reece."

Reece raked his fingers through his hair. "I know." He heaved a deep breath. "I'm pretty surprised myself." His next sigh was powerful enough to puff out his cheeks.

Finally, Derrick was able to ask a serious question. "What about Jeff?"

"Yeah, Reece," Jason added. "If this woman's in some kind of trouble, is it possible that she'll drag you and Jeff into it?"

Reece had thought long and hard about his eight-year-old son. Jeff was his main priority in life. He loved the child, and he'd never do anything that might jeopardize Jeff's safety.

"Well," Reece said, "Jeff will be at summer camp until the weekend after next—"

"Oh, right," Derrick said. "Timmy did tell me that Jeff was going to camp." He shook his head, grinning. "Tim was pretty bummed out about not being old enough to go this year."

"So—" Jason directed his comment at Reece "—that gives you less than two weeks to solve this woman's problem and get her out of your house."

The waitress approached their table. "You fellas ready for another round?"

"Sure, Gale," Jason said. "But just one more, then I gotta be going. Gina's got the sniffles, poor thing, and Katie's watching her for me. I shouldn't stay much 'onger."

Reece and Derrick both nodded.

"Reece—" Derrick leaned toward his friend, his countenance the epitome of sincere concern "—you know, don't you, that this lady you've got staying in your spare bedroom is probably *hiding something*."

The final two words had Jason clamping his hand over his mouth to try to stifle a laugh.

"Very funny," Reece said with not a hint of humor in his voice.

The other two men finally surrendered to their laughter. Reece suffered through it, knowing that Derrick's ribbing wasn't meant to hurt his feelings. Derrick was only repeating the very warning Reece himself had given to both of his friends. Reece had warned Derrick about Anna's intentions all those months ago.

And now Anna was Derrick's wife, a tiny voice reminded Reece.

Reece had even warned Jason about Katie just a few short weeks ago. He wanted desperately to point out that he'd been dead right where Katie was concerned—she had been hiding her true identity from Jason. But he refused to lower himself to his friends' level by bringing it up. Besides, Jason and Katie had seemed to work things out so well, what with the fact that they were up to their necks in wedding plans. Yes, he decided, things were okay between them.

So far, the tiny voice negatively intoned.

The trouble with Maggie Dunlap, Reece told himself as he silently got back to the matter at hand, was that he felt certain she *was* hiding something—that she wasn't being entirely honest about this trouble she was having. She must have some idea of who was playing these devious games. As soon as he got home, he would demand that she open up and tell him everything she knew or suspected. He couldn't possibly help her if she didn't open up and be completely honest, he reasoned.

"Yep," Jason joked, "in Reece's estimation, every woman in the *world* is up to something!"

"Look, guys," Reece said. "I don't have to sit here and take this."

He knew the guys were just trying to get under his skin about his helping Maggie. And if he weren't so preoccupied with the woman, he would probably even enjoy their good-natured ribbing. But he simply had too much on his mind.

Reece felt utterly baffled by the sheer magnetism that seemed to draw him toward her. Every time he'd been alone with her—in his office last week, earlier today at her house and, most especially, tonight in the guest bedroom of his own home—there had been some force, some powerful energy that had captivated his attention. She'd felt it, too; he'd read it in her eyes, heard it in her strained voice. Luckily, this meeting with his friends had given him the perfect excuse to bolt.

Hell, the very last thing he needed was a woman messing up his life!

The waitress set down three bottles of beer on the table along with their check before hurrying to the next table to take an order.

"And if this Maggie Dunlap is as distrusting of the opposite sex as you say she is," Derrick said to Reece between chuckles, "then the two of you are like two peas in a pod."

"All right, that's it," Reece proclaimed. "I've taken enough ribbing about this. I'm outta here."

He pushed his chair back, tossed some bills on the table and headed for the door.

"Aw, I think we made him mad," Jason said.

Derrick nodded his head. "I think you're right."

For one brief moment on the way to the door, Reece's chaotic mind calmed and he nearly chuckled when he heard Jason shoot back, "But since it looks like he *is* leaving, I've got dibs on his beer."

"Hey—"

The sound of Derrick hailing him had Reece glancing back toward the table.

"You're not using our little joking session here as an excuse to get mad, are you? So you can run home to Maggie?"

The angry scowl that filled Reece's face was genuine.

"Hell, no!" he roared. He pushed his way out the door and into the parking lot, his friends' laughter echoing in his ears all the way to his car.

Maggie stretched in the padded lounge chair, luxuriating in cool, salt-scented morning breeze coming off the bay. She'd slept well last night, awoken refreshed for the first time in…she couldn't remember how many days.

The expanse of blue-green water before her lent a serene quality to the morning; however, that was only one of the reasons Maggie felt in such a good mood. Another was the safe haven that Reece had provided her with. She'd literally slept like a babe.

"Good morning."

She smiled up at Reece as he came through the French door and joined her on the deck outside.

"Hi," she said.

Rather than a business suit, today he wore olive-colored casual dress pants and a striped, short-sleeved cotton shirt. He looked good, she noted before dragging her eyes back up to his freshly shaved face. And his cologne, a scent reminiscent of hot and spicy nights, smelled wonderful.

Obviously, he noticed her appraisal of him, and she felt her face grow warm.

"It's Friday," he said, explaining his less formal attire. "Everyone follows the office custom of dressing down on the last work day of the week."

Maggie nodded.

"I've got coffee brewing. You ready for a cup?"

"That'd be great," she told him, making to stand.

"No, no." He stayed her with a light touch on her shoulder. "I'll get it. What do you take?"

Maggie relaxed. "Just a little cream."

He disappeared into the house, and she marveled at how the spot he'd touched on her shoulder seemed to grow warmer by the second. Closing her eyes, she sighed. She couldn't allow herself to react to this man. It was silly. Was she experiencing some sick psychological illness? She'd heard of twisted stories where abductees fell for their kidnappers....

However, she hadn't been abducted, and Reece was no kidnapper. He was a generous man who had offered her sanctuary.

But did that really matter? her mind argued. He was a man! And the men she investigated were proof that relationships weren't worth the effort they took to cultivate. If that wasn't enough to convince her, there were always her memories of Peter—

Maggie forcefully shut the door on those dark thoughts. The morning was much to bright and beautiful to be clouding the day with such black and shadowy musings.

These feelings she was experiencing toward Reece were like weeds in the well-tended garden of her life. She might not understand them, but she didn't need to. What was necessary was that she rip them up by the roots, before they had a chance to spread.

Reece came back out onto the deck. "Here you go."

The task of accepting the steaming mug of coffee from him without touching his hand was impossible. The instant her palm brushed against the backs of his fingers, Maggie felt as if she'd been jolted with a small electric charge. She gripped the mug, the aftershock running the length of her arm and through her body, settling somewhere near her solar plexus.

Blinking, she focused every ounce of her attention on the coffee and the rich-scented tendrils of steam rising from it.

"Mmm. Smells good." She worked hard to keep her voice neutral, unemotional.

Get a grip, she silently demanded of herself.

"I came in early last night." Reece took a seat in the chair next to hers. "I was hoping to talk to you, but you'd already gone to bed."

"Yeah," Maggie said, "I guess yesterday really wiped me out."

As he sipped his coffee, he glanced at his watch. "I have a few minutes before I have to leave for the office. Do you mind if we talk?"

"I don't mind at all."

Reece hesitated a moment, then said, "I thought we should discuss our plans."

"Our plans?"

"Mmm-hmm." He rested his elbow on the chair's armrest.

Maggie helplessly darted a quick glance at the corded muscles of his tanned forearms.

"We need to come up with some way to find out who's been breaking into your home."

"I can't let you get involved in this," she said, forcing herself to look into his face.

Reece chuckled, and even though she knew she had to remain on guard, she had to admit she liked the rich resonance of it.

"Don't you think I'm already involved?" he asked.

She had to smile. "Well, I don't want you becoming any more embroiled in my problems than you already are."

"That's silly," he told her. "You said yourself you don't have anyone else to turn to." His voice grew rough as he added, "Besides, I'd like to help you catch this creep. I hate the idea of someone preying on defenseless women—"

"I am *not* a defenseless woman," she said, cutting him off. "I may have been frightened. I may have even cried. But that does not make me defenseless—or weak—in *any* sense of the word."

Shocked by how quickly her anger had consumed her, she fumed in the silence. The awkwardness that had suddenly sprung up between them stretched out as neither one of them spoke. The fact that he didn't apologize for his stupid remark only irritated her more because it meant he really believed the hogwash that had just come out of his mouth.

Maggie stood up. But before she could go into the house—before she could leave his asinine presence—he stopped her by reaching out and grasping her wrist.

She steeled herself. However, when his skin made contact with hers, she was rocked by the sensation that coursed through her entire body. She wanted to jerk her arm away, but something in his eyes restrained her. Some strong magnetic force had her gaze locked on his.

"Sit down, Maggie," he said. "Please. Drink your coffee."

Slowly, she lowered herself into the seat and laced the fingers of both hands around the mug.

She didn't know why she wasn't telling this man exactly what she thought of him and his views of *defenseless women*. Normally, she would have reamed out any man who would dare suggest she was anything but a strong, intelligent, independent woman.

The coffee didn't seem to have any taste at all as she sipped and swallowed.

"Do you have any idea at all who is doing this?" he asked.

Her ire continued to smolder as she debated whether or not to answer him. His opinion where females were concerned might be idiotic, but the man *had* offered her a place to stay when she had nowhere else to go. For that reason alone, he deserved an answer of some kind.

Finally, she relented. "Yes," she said. "I think it's the husband of one of my clients. His name's Buster. He's an uneducated chauvinist." She grimaced. "And I'm being quite kind in my description. His he-man mentality would lend itself perfectly to the stunts being pulled on me."

"I see." He gazed out at the bay for a moment, then his dark eyes were on her once more. "So what do you propose we do?"

"*We?*" She couldn't keep the incredulity out of her tone. "*We* are going to do nothing. *I* am going to get pictures of my client's husband, hopefully with his mistress, and then I'll deliver them to his wife. After that, the bad news will be out in the open, and there should be no need for the man to bother me any longer."

Reece's mahogany eyes homed in on her, dark and intense. "I don't like the idea that you'll be out there actually seeking out the weirdo who is doing his damnedest to terrify you."

Her gaze was drawn to the lines of worry bracketing his mouth.

"I really would prefer to go with you." After a moment's hesitation, he added, "So, what time did you want to leave tonight?"

Maggie realized that, in insinuating that he go with her, he was inferring that she couldn't take care of herself. Such a suggestion made by anyone—especially a man—would normally have made her furious. And yes, his ridiculous statement regarding defenseless women had irritated her. However, there was something almost...nice about his offer to join her on the stakeout. Something that had her feeling safe and secure.

As she studied him in silence, the attraction that welled up between them was about as subtle as a two-by-four right between the eyes.

The fierce pounding of her heart sent blood whooshing through her ears, and she felt as though she couldn't get enough oxygen into her lungs. Her mouth went dry, and her eyes darted from his, to the ultrasexy smile crease at one corner of his mouth, to the firm line of his jaw and back up to his gaze.

She couldn't believe how drawn she was to Reece Newton. It was almost as if the laws of physics had somehow become skewed, and gravity was pulling, pulling at her—not down, but *toward* him!

Ignore it, she silently commanded. Ignore it and it will definitely go away.

However "nice" it was to have Reece's concern, she couldn't allow herself to depend on anyone for her safety. She couldn't allow herself to be protected. She had to be totally independent. And she certainly couldn't allow herself to give in to this attraction she felt. Not after what she saw every day and every night on her job. The lying, the cheating, the pain, hurt and humiliation. And certainly not after her experience with Peter.

Yet she didn't want to injure the man's feelings.

"Reece—" she reached out and touched him on the forearm "—I *do* appreciate your offer to come along. But this is my job. It's my problem."

A tiny smile sauntered across his mouth, and Maggie felt her heart skip several beats. Why did the man have to be so darned gorgeous?

"I think you've forgotten something," he said, his wine-warm voice quiet and steady. "You have no car."

The dismal reality of his words sunk into her head.

His smile widened wickedly. "So, like I said, what time did you want to leave tonight?"

Chapter Four

"I can't believe I actually talked my way into this."

Maggie chuckled at Reece's groaning complaint.

"Surveillance work could never be described as glamorous," she commented. "It involves a lot of waiting and watching—" she grinned at him across the dark interior of the car "—and then more waiting and watching."

They were parked on the narrow dirt shoulder of a road that, although paved with asphalt, barely made it into the tertiary category. Maggie glanced into her binoculars toward the dimly lit doorway of the Candy Bar, a run-down roadhouse patronized by a rowdy motorcycle gang.

"I never knew such a place existed in Bayview," Reece had said when they first arrived.

She had told him he would be surprised to know how some people chose to entertain themselves after the sun went down. And she'd been amused by his disapproving attitude when he'd discovered this wasn't the first time she had staked out the Candy Bar in an effort to get the pictures she needed for her client.

"Sometimes it takes several weeks of watching—"

"And waiting," he'd interjected.

She had laughed. "Yes, and waiting to gather the evidence my clients are paying me to get. But don't worry, the place closes down at two. These people may like to carouse at night, but they'll be heading home soon. Most of them have respectable day jobs."

"And how do you know that?"

A tiny grin had pulled at one corner of her lips. "Research."

He'd been quiet a moment. "I can see how this job could be dangerous."

Deep concern had laced his comment—a deep concern Maggie refused to allow herself to appreciate.

"I've been doing this a long time," she had told him. "I can take care of myself."

But then he'd pushed the issue, and feeling her irritation flare, Maggie had suggested that they both quiet down and do the job they had come to do. That had been over ninety minutes ago, and the annoyance she'd experienced at Reece's overbearing concern had long since dissolved in the silence of the darkened car. Now Reece's grumbling protest regarding his current predicament had a grin tugging at her lips, another chuckle just waiting at the back of her throat.

"Why on earth do you do this? What was it that steered you onto this career path?"

His questions faded the smile from her face like caustic bleach faded the blue from denim jeans. However, she was surprised that his query didn't anger her.

"I don't mind talking," she told him. "But I think it would be better if we stuck to safer topics."

Moonlight filtered into the car, throwing shadows

across his handsome face. He studied her, then he slowly bobbed his head.

"Anything's better than sitting in silence," he said.

"Tell me more about Jeff."

She sensed his soft smile the instant she mentioned his son's name.

"I've already told you that he's the center of my world."

"You have custody." She spoke the words as a statement, but she hoped it would urge him to elaborate about himself—about his past, and even more specifically, about his divorce. She couldn't deny the curiosity burning inside her. And it wasn't something he'd told her about before.

"Yeah," he said. "Jeffrey and I have been going it alone since he was just a toddler."

"I think it's very admirable that you're raising him on—"

"And why is that?"

His abrupt interruption made her go silent, and she stared at him in the dim moonlight.

"Why should it be admirable that I'm raising my son?" he pushed. "I'm his father. He's my responsibility."

"Hey, I didn't mean to press a button. All I'm trying to say is that, normally, in most divorces…" she stammered, "it's the woman who…who takes custody of the children. Especially young children."

Thoughts flew through her head as she scrambled to explain. She certainly hadn't meant to upset him in any way. Whatever his beef was with his ex, he sure was prickly where the custody issue was concerned.

"Yeah, well," Reece fairly growled, "a woman has to want her child in order to request custody. Not that I would have given Jeff up without a battle, in any case."

"Your wife—or rather, your ex—didn't want her own son?"

What kind of woman would have a baby she didn't want? Maggie wondered. She simply couldn't imagine any woman having a baby and then not fighting to the death for custody when her marriage went sour. What terrible thing had Reece done to hurt his wife to the point that she hadn't even put up a fight for her son?

"Look," Reece said quietly, "talking about my ex-wife isn't something that comes easy for me. Can we switch gears here?"

"Sure."

So, her curiosity wasn't going to be satiated; her questions were going to remain unanswered. Still, she couldn't help wondering what he'd done to ruin his marriage....

What if hadn't been his fault?

It was *always* the man's fault, an emphatic voice piped up from somewhere in the back of her brain. She had witnessed it in case after case, devastated client after devastated client.

But what if...?

The question lingered in her mind. And suddenly, she had the oddest sensation, the strangest urge to reach out to him—in more than just the physical sense of the word. She wanted to understand him. She wanted to hear his and Jeff's story. But most of all she wanted to comfort him, touch him, caress away the bitterness that had been the thick underlining of his tone when he'd spoken of his son's mother.

The heavy scent of honeysuckle had seeped through the partially open window to waft all around them, thick and sweet. Maggie assumed the aroma had been there all along, but she hadn't noticed it until just this moment. The summer air was warm, but she didn't think that had anything at all to do with the fact that she felt the sudden need to concentrate on pulling it, deeply and evenly, into her lungs. She stared at him in the silent darkness, her heart thudding against her rib cage. The attraction between them hummed a lingering chord that refused to be ignored.

"So," he began, his whisper-soft voice like a caress, "what are we going to do about this?"

Her eyes flew open wide. "About what?"

His face was shrouded in shadow, but a swath of pale moonlight illuminated his eyes. The expression she saw reflected in his gaze, along with his acute silence and upraised brows, told her in no uncertain terms that he knew that she knew exactly to what he was referring.

With her pulse pounding in her ears, she let her eyes trail along the dashboard. Heat suffused her face, and she was grateful to be sitting in the dark.

She had realized she was attracted to this man. She'd even realized the magnitude of what she felt—hadn't she likened it to a living, breathing *thing?* But the fact that he'd so bluntly brought it out into the open like this was overwhelming.

Thoughts and words scrambled around in her head. What should she say? How should she respond?

Well, she finally told herself, if he could be so blunt and honest, so could she.

"Reece," she said softly, unable to look directly at him, "I'm not interested in a...relationship. It's not that—"

"Hell, that's a good thing," he cut her off. "'Cause a relationship is the furthest thing from my mind."

Her gaze darted to his face, a frown biting deeply into her brow. Confusion inundated her mind as she wondered how she should feel about his statement, how she should respond.

Then he chuckled.

The warm, silky rumble soothed away her frown and even churned up an urge to place her flattened palm against his chest to feel the vibration, but she was still totally bewildered about exactly where this conversation was leading.

"It's pretty obvious," he went on, "that there's something going on here."

This time, the reverberation that emanated from deep in his chest was even lower, even sexier, and Maggie felt her heart kick into high gear.

She heard the sensuous grin in his voice as he said, "I mean, I don't know if you've noticed, but I'm *hot* for you, Maggie."

She stifled a gasp. Without thinking, she reached up and tugged nervously at a short, curling lock of hair right behind her ear. "Look, Reece," she began slowly, her voice hoarse, "since neither one of us is looking to get involved, then maybe we should just try to…to look the other way."

His head tilted a fraction. "Look the other way?" he asked.

She licked her lips. She swallowed. How could she explain what she meant without seeming incredibly naive?

"Maybe we should try to pretend…" She let the sentence fade. "Maybe we should…" Again, she faltered. Then she gave it one last attempt. "Maybe we should try to, ah, to…ignore what it is we're…feeling."

The air in the tiny space seemed to compact, intensify.

"Why on earth would we want to do that?"

His wholly carnal tone sent a sensuous shiver coursing across her skin. Her nipples tightened painfully against the fabric of her shirt, and again, she was extremely thankful for the camouflage of darkness.

Dear Lord, how she wanted this man! Never in her life had she felt such a strong, reckless, purely physical *need*. How could she feel this irresistible attraction to a man she barely knew? And how could it be that, at this moment, the attraction pulsing between them seemed to define her very existence?

Knowing that Reece was sharing the same feelings only served to heighten this need that plagued her so deliciously.

He rested his arm along the back of the seat and trailed his fingers along her shoulders. With both hands, she gripped the binoculars that lay on her lap. Her eyelids lowered, and she reveled in the feel of his warm skin against her neck. He fingered the same short lock of her hair that she had a habit of tugging, curling it gently around his thumb.

Her inhalation was shaky and difficult, and it seemed that the temperature in the car had heated up several degrees in as many seconds. Oddly, her entire body tensed and relaxed at the same time, and only with great effort could she open her eyes.

She focused on his handsome face as he slowly leaned closer and closer. His silken breath caressed her cheek. He was going to kiss her, she realized, a delighted shiver coursing through her body.

Soft. Warm. Gentle. The initial sensations crowded out all thought from her mind. His lips skimmed across hers, his tongue tentatively tasting, teasing. In a wholly natural and unwitting reaction, she signed against his mouth. The binoculars that lay in her lap slipped to the floor, forgotten, as she slid her palms up his broad chest.

The hammering of his heart excited her, telling her he

was as swept away as she was. He planted tiny kisses along her jawline, stopping to nibble on the delicate lobe of her ear. The heated summer air became impossible to breathe, and she felt her chest rise and fall raggedly.

He smelled of heady spices, the warm, erotically male scent of him wafting around her, ever deepening the desire surging through her.

"You smell like summer rain."

Reece whispered the words against her ear, and she marveled at how in tune their thoughts seemed to be.

His lips brushed her cheekbone, her brow. "And you taste...delicious."

With her mind a jumble of sensations, feelings, urges and splintered thoughts, Maggie was actually surprised when she was able to notice how his breathing had become as ragged as her own. A sharp spear of distress momentarily pierced her consciousness when she realized he was the one getting to do all the tasting.

She ran her fingers over the firm muscles of his biceps and then along his strong shoulders. Tilting her head to one side, she proceeded to do a little savoring of her own.

His skin was luscious, bringing to mind dark and heated mysteries. With her first kiss, he raised his chin a fraction, giving her free rein. To most men, this would have seemed a submissive gesture; however, Reece seemed all the more masculine as he silently invited Maggie to explore.

She rained kisses on his corded throat, along his jaw and, finally, she pressed her moist lips to his. Her name spilled from his mouth in a tattered whisper, and Maggie felt the desire inside her coil and churn like molten lava.

Her heart pounded. Her blood surged. Maggie was ready. More than anything else on the face of the earth, she wanted to propel the kiss to a deeper, more intimate level. With every intention of urging Reece on, she threaded her fingers through his hair, and parted her lips for him.

She heard his groan, tasted the sound of it.

"Maggie."

A whimper nearly escaped her when he pulled back, but she held it in check. She tugged him toward her.

"Maggie, wait," he said.

Her silent gaze was filled with frantic questions.

Reece's dark eyes studied her for one brief, regret-filled moment. Then he said, "Look."

When he lifted his head to look out the window toward the bar, she let her eyes follow. Three people were exiting the building.

"It's him." Lament was clear in her tone, and her brain still felt languid and fuzzed over with the passion that had taken over every thought, every breath, every movement. But she had a job to do. She was a professional.

The small thought was powerful enough to clear her mind completely.

"It's Buster." This time, her voice was strong and plainly reflected the idea that she was a woman on a mission.

She shoved herself from Reece's embrace, and she automatically reached for the binoculars.

"Thanks for keeping an eye out," she murmured, mentally kicking herself when she realized how easy it would have been to miss the man she'd come here seeking.

Then another thought flashed through her mind—given Reece's position with his back to the bar, keeping watch must have been physically awkward for him. She'd been so involved in their kiss, a freight train could have barreled by and she wouldn't have noticed. However, Reece had succeeded in kissing her with mind-numbing intensity *and* keeping one eye on the door of the bar. He certainly couldn't have been as involved in the intimate encounter as she had been.

Somehow, the idea embarrassed her. But she didn't have time to think about that now. Scrambling to her knees, she inched closer toward Reece and the driver-side window, planting her knee smack in his lap.

Her brain barely registered his startled "Oomph" as she raised the binoculars and peered across the road.

"It *is* him," she confirmed.

"Would you kindly remove your knee from my groin?"

She lowered the binoculars a couple of inches and blinked. Then she looked down.

"Sorry," she murmured, and hastened to position her bent knee on the seat next to his thigh.

Her quarry stood right outside the bar, across the expanse of pothole-ridden parking lot, and she knew she should be watching him closely. However, Reece was so near. Near enough that she could easily have tipped up her chin and planted a light kiss on his jaw.

Focus, damn it! her mind railed at her. He obviously hadn't been as swept away as you thought!

Now, just wait a minute, her logical brain argued. Would you have wanted Buster to leave the bar unnoticed? Would you have wanted Reece to have become so wrapped up in you that the entire evening's work was ruined?

The woman in her whispered a stubborn yes to both questions; however, the professional investigator in her shouted a hearty no.

Confusion clouded her thoughts. What was the matter with her?

You have a job to do here, the logical voice reminded her sternly.

"I have a job to do here," she repeated, sure that once she heard the words spoken aloud her muscles and tendons would move to do her bidding.

"Then by all means," Reece said, "do it."

But his silky tone conveyed in no uncertain terms that there was something else he wanted to do—something very particular—and it had nothing whatsoever to do with spying on some motorcycle-riding, beer-belly-toting jerk who might or might not be cheating on his wife. Heaven help her, but the urge to kiss him was still very strong.

"Ree-eece!" Feeling flattered at his teasing, she gave him a gentle nudge on the shoulder. A wide grin was his only response. "I have to do this," she said. "I'm almost certain that this is the guy who's been coming into my house."

The reminder immediately knocked some seriousness into Reece's attitude. He sat up straighter, reaching for the binoculars.

"You're sure this is your man? He's got two other people with him. One's a female." He hesitated a moment. "The other's a male, tall, thin."

"Yeah," Maggie said, concentrating on the scene before her. "I'm sure it's him. I've followed Buster before. I'm hoping that the woman crawls onto the back of *his* bike and not the other guy's."

She reached into the back seat of Reece's car, tugging on the strap of her heavy camera case. After unzipping the case, she pulled out the 35 mm camera with its huge telephoto night lens.

Maggie snapped several pictures. Then she stopped and just watched the man through the camera's lens. He laughed with the other two people there with him, and

Maggie felt a flash of unadulterated fury to think that this was the man who had invaded her home, who had terrorized her for the pure fun of it.

"What I'd like to do," she murmured, her voice tight with anger, "is pull that metal-studded leather vest over his head and kick his—"

"All right," Reece gently admonished her. "Calm down. You need to keep a clear head."

Maggie watched the man move to the row of motorcycles. His was a fancy low-riding one, all glossy black paint and shiny chrome. He kick-started the bike, its *pug-pug-pug* growing louder as he revved the engine with a sharp twist of his wrist.

"Looks like she's with the other guy," Reece observed.

Disappointment welled up in Maggie as she watched the woman snake her fingers through the thin man's hair. The kiss she planted on his lips was passionate and possessive.

There was no doubt about it. The woman and the thin man were a couple.

"Shoot," Maggie complained. And she heaved a sigh as she lowered the camera.

Reece continued to watch through the binoculars. "What do you know about him?"

"Buster?"

He nodded.

"Everything except what I need to know," she told him dismally. But before she could expound on her statement, Reece's whispered curse had her looking out the window.

"I think we've been spotted," he said.

Adrenaline, hot and acidic, surged through Maggie's body. With a careful hand, she hastily replaced the cap on the telephoto lens and tucked her camera on the floor behind the front seat.

She didn't even bother to look out the window—she could hear the motorcycle coming closer with each passing second. Instead, she used the time to develop a quick plan.

"Hurry," she said, twisting around and wedging her bottom in the tight space between Reece and the steering wheel.

After his initial gasp of total surprise, he said, "Would you kindly tell me what you think—" he gasped again, this time in pain, as she tried to force her butt onto his lap "—you're doing? Ouch!"

"Do you think I'm enjoying this? Let me in here," she demanded breathlessly. "We can pretend we're on a date. Engaged in some heavy petting."

Immediately, Reece slid one hand under her derriere and began firmly pushing her off him. "As much as I'd like to play this game with you, Maggie," he said in between grunts of exertion, "I have no intention of allowing us to get caught like a cork in a bottle when we may need some freedom of movement. I might have to punch this guy in the nose before this is all over."

Finally, Maggie found herself shoved none too gently back over to the passenger side of the front seat.

"Oh, don't worry about that." She straightened her blouse, trying to gather a bit of her dignity.

By this time, the man had parked his bike directly in front of Reece's car and was approaching them on foot.

"This guy's only man enough to terrorize women," Maggie commented.

The leather-clad biker walked up to Reece's partially opened window.

"Let's hope you're right," Reece said softly to Maggie.

His gaze swung around to the burly man standing outside the car, and Maggie could sense the instant birth of

Reece's hostility. He pushed open the door, forcing the biker back several paces.

"Hey, buddy, how about stepping away from the car?" Reece said to the man. As he was talking, Reece pushed himself out of the seat and into the heated summer night.

Now alone in the car, Maggie muttered, "Just like a man to go full speed ahead with all that testosterone-induced aggression."

"The name's Buster, man," the biker said. "And you don't need to get all bent out of shape. I only came over here to see what was going on. What the hell are you two doin' out here, anyway?"

"What's it to you?"

Maggie actually groaned at the challenge in Reece's voice. She decided she'd better do something—now—before Reece *did* start a fight.

She opened the passenger-side door and got out of the car. "Hey, mister," she called to Buster. "Can't a woman get her man...alone."

She turned a sickeningly suggestive gaze onto Reece.

"Oh, ah..." Buster stammered, "I, ah, certainly didn't mean to intrude."

He started to turn away from them, then he suddenly stopped, his eyes narrowing as they homed in on something inside the car. Maggie felt her blood pulsing, and she dipped her head to see what the biker was looking at.

The binoculars! Reece had left them sitting out on the front seat in plain view.

"You two ain't out here makin' out," Buster said, looking across the hood of the car at Maggie. "I mighta just had a birthday, but it wasn't my first one. You guys are out here spying on somebody—"

He stopped as though a blunt-tipped revelation had just

whacked him on the back of the head. One of his eyes narrowed to a slit.

"You're that bitch what talked Sally into leaving me, ain't cha?"

Reece's reaction was lightning fast. Before Maggie could even draw a quick breath to stop him, he'd slammed his car door shut, closed the gap between himself and Buster and grabbed a handful of the biker's leather vest in his fist.

"Watch what you call the lady."

The steely tone of Reece's voice made Maggie's insides quiver with fear. She saw the same emotion reflected in Buster's eyes. Nobody moved for several moments.

Finally, Buster raised his hands in a palms-out, surrendering gesture.

"I got no argument with you, man," he told Reece.

Reece released his hold on Buster's vest. The biker took a backward step.

"Hey, Buster," the thin man across the street called out. "You need some help, man?"

"No thanks, Chug," Buster yelled back. "I'm okay. Everything's okay." Then he turned back to Reece. "It's *her*, man." Buster pointed in Maggie's general direction without making eye contact. "She talked my wife into leavin' me. She filled Sally's head so full of lies. She told my wife that I was screwing around on her, man."

Maggie couldn't believe the drivel coming out of this man's mouth.

"I wouldn't advise you to be hanging out with her," Buster continued his diatribe. The man's tone lowered an octave, as though he'd suddenly become Reece's best buddy, a close confidant wanting to bestow some serious, well-meaning, man-to-man advice as he said, "Man, she's trouble with a capital *T*."

After a moment, Reece responded with a soft "Thanks for the warning."

Maggie frowned, unable to discern exactly what Reece meant by his statement. Had he meant to be facetious? she wondered. However, she hadn't detected even a smidgen of sarcasm in his tone. Reece couldn't possibly have meant that as an expression of appreciation. Or could he have? Was it possible that he actually believed what this balding, beer-bellied jerk was saying about her?

"Because of *her*—" Buster indicated Maggie with a small, sharp jerk of his head "—Sally left me. My wife would never have left the house on her own. We've been together for over twenty-two years. Sally would never have moved out. But this bitc—" He stopped himself. "This broad convinced my wife to leave me. She tried to bust up my marriage, man. And everything she told Sally was a low-down, dirty *lie*. I have never cheated on my Sally. She's my woman. We might argue a little now and again, but I'd never cheat on her."

Reece studied the aging man standing in front of him. Was that really pity he felt twisting in his gut? The bumps and knocks of Buster's obvious "live hard, die young" attitude toward life had certainly taken a heavy toll on the man. But how a person chose to live his life was nobody's business but his own. And no matter what a person's lifestyle, he deserved to have his marriage treated with utmost sanctity. So who the heck did Maggie think she was to talk this man's wife into moving out of their home? Especially when Maggie had admitted that she hadn't yet actually caught Buster cheating on his wife.

Something mingled with the pity wrenching in his stomach, and he finally identified it as suspicion and outrage directed at Maggie. When he glanced across the car at her, he knew very well that there was serious accusation in his eyes.

There was blatant hurt in hers. He could read it as clear as a cloudless sky. But he ignored it. No one should take it upon him- or herself to break up a marriage. The close bond between a husband and wife should only be shattered by the man and woman directly involved in the relationship.

The hurt reflected in her gaze turned to anger, and her shoulders squared as she quietly asked, "You don't actually believe this bull he's feeding you, do you?"

"Well," he began, "did you talk his wife into leaving?"

Her chin tipped up. "Not only did I talk Sally into leaving, I drove her to the women's shelter myself."

The outrage he felt swelled like a tidal wave. "Why would you do such a thing? You had no evidence that this man had a mistress. You told me yourself, you hadn't caught him cheating on his wife." His eyes narrowed. "I'm sorry, Maggie, but what you did was wrong."

Fury shot from her like a laser beam, spearing him straight through the heart.

"How dare you judge me," she said. "You have no idea—"

She halted, and he watched as she took a purposeful deep breath. Her anger had her actually trembling—her delicate features were hard, her green gaze icy cold.

Once she'd gotten herself under control, she said, "I told Sally she'd be better off without her husband. And I did drive her to the shelter—but only after I made a quick stop at the emergency room. You see, Buster here used his wife as a human punching bag. She had a black eye, a swollen jaw and a broken finger that needed to be treated. But it seems that being beaten to within an inch of her life wasn't reason enough for Sally to leave this wonderful man. I had to promise to get some pictures of him with another woman." Her frigid gaze swept over to the biker. *"Cheating—"* she spit out the word "—now there's a good reason to leave a man."

A deep sense of contrition dragged on Reece's shoulders like fifty-pound weights. Maggie had had good reason to urge Sally to leave her husband.

Reece remembered something Maggie had said earlier when they realized they had been spotted by the man they were spying on. She'd said Buster was only man enough to terrorize women. Reece had thought she'd been talking about the fearful situation she'd been facing regarding the intruder in her home—but now he believed Maggie had been commenting on the biker's treatment of his wife.

Anger exploded inside him like a stick of dynamite. In his estimation, there was nothing worse than a woman-beater. Reece's eyes narrowed at Buster.

"Hey, man…" Sensing he was about to lose Reece's sympathy, the biker took a backward step toward his motorcycle. "You know how it is." His voice was jovial and once again held that good-buddy intonation. "Sally was bad-mouthin' me, man. A woman needs to be knocked into line now and again. Yours could use a little—"

The rest of the man's sentence was choked off as Reece grabbed him up short by his leather vest.

"I'm going to tell you something for your own good, Buster," Reece growled out. "And you'd better listen up. You stay away from Maggie. And if you *ever* come near her house again, I will find you and personally kick your—"

"I don't know what you're talkin' about, man," Buster blubbered. "I never went near your woman. I ain't been messin' with her. And I have no idea where she lives. You got the wrong man."

Reece was so close to Buster that he could smell the stench of stale beer on his breath.

"I guess you're right," Reece said. "Because from what I see, you don't even fit the description of a man." He gave the biker a shove. "Get the hell out of here," Reece said. "You make me sick."

Buster nearly fell as he stumbled to his bike. He straddled the Harley and kick-started the engine. "In case you're interested," he said, his tone suddenly cocky as though having something powerful between his legs restored some small portion of his lost dignity, "Sally came home today." The grin he tossed at Maggie could have been described as a sneer. "So consider yourself fired."

He roared off into the night, his bike loud enough to wake the dead.

Reece's exhalation was forceful. He needed to apologize to Maggie for questioning her actions, and he needed to do it now. However, when he looked over at her, he frowned at the anger that seemed to pulse off of her like a hot, heavy beat.

"Listen—"

"You don't want to talk to me right now," she warned ominously. "I'm furious with you, I'm furious with Sally—and I'm not even going to get paid for all these hours I sat out here tonight." She dragged trembling fingers through her short hair. "I'm so angry, I could spit nails." Maggie opened her door. "Just get me out of here."

With that, she got into the car, leaving him standing alone in the darkness.

Chapter Five

Reece didn't even see the lush, green scenery as he drove north along Chesapeake Bay toward Camp Kimmiwun to visit his son Jeff. Thoughts of Maggie crowded out everything else from his mind. Reece should have been contemplating and anticipating spending this beautiful summer Saturday with Jeff, but the woman who had invaded his home now invaded his brain, as well.

She'd refused to speak to him since the stakeout. He had tried several times to broach the subject, to apologize for his behavior, but Maggie had cut him to the quick with a silent glare. He knew if she could, she'd leave his home. But lack of money and mode of transportation kept her stranded. And he was happy about that, because having her in his house was the only way he could protect her.

He and Maggie might not be on speaking terms in real life; however, his dreams were another story altogether. His nights had been filled with ecstasy…and agony.

The taste of her honeyed lips had been pure paradise,

and in his dreams, he'd kissed them again and again. His fingertips had trailed, night after night, along the soft, satin curves of her flesh, and her husky, audible reaction to his touch was enough to drive him stark raving mad. The memory was so vivid in his mind that, even now, his body instantly reacted, and he shifted in the seat to relieve the pressure of his desire for her.

However, the agony always came. Time and again. Just when he and Maggie were about to surrender completely to the ravenous passion that seemed to utterly eat them alive—he would awaken. He'd sit up in bed, his heart racing, his body tense and wanting, his skin covered with a sheen of sweat. Reece had decided that there was no worse agony that could ever be endured.

Until, in the light of day, he suffered her silence.

What bothered him most was the fact that her anger had seemed to dissipate, leaving behind a huge amount of hurt feelings. Her anger he could have dealt with, but the insult and pain he read in her eyes made him feel terribly guilty. So guilty, in fact, that he'd taken it upon himself to arrange to have her car towed to a garage and repaired. He'd paid for it himself. Oh, *she* didn't know that. He was certain Maggie Dunlap was too proud and too angry to accept his money.

He expected to be repaid eventually. Once Maggie discovered who had damaged her car, and once she felt safe from that person, she could notify the police, and Reece would be free to fill out the paperwork to make a claim against her car insurance. But right now, he felt it best to simply let her assume the insurance company had taken care of the car repairs. And if he was never repaid, then that was okay, too. He would just chalk it up as a small penance to pay for having thought the worst of her.

Reece had gained a great deal of respect for Maggie

that night. She had done all she could for Buster's wife, Sally. And knowing that her client had gone back home to her wife-beating husband probably worried Maggie a lot. Of course, this was just an assumption on Reece's part. Maggie hadn't confided in him. She was much too angry for that.

He shook his head, silently vowing once again to fix things between himself and Maggie as soon as he got home this evening.

Turning onto the tree-lined country road that led to the camp, Reece focused his thoughts on his son. He hoped Jeff was having a good time at Camp Kimmiwun.

The counselors taught the children to canoe and fish; they swam in the bay, practiced shooting with bows and arrows and told old Chippewa folk tales around a campfire each evening. The privately owned and operated camp prided itself on enhancing youngsters' knowledge of the Native American culture that had once abounded on the Chesapeake peninsula. In fact, the very name of the camp, Kimmiwun, came from the Algonquian Indian word meaning "rain." Reece felt a ghost of a smile tugging on his lips as he remembered the camp director remarking that rain was one thing the campers hoped they didn't see during their stay.

As Reece passed through the wide wooden gates of the camp, his smile broadened. He'd been busy with Maggie and her problems over the past few days, but Reece realized suddenly just how much he'd missed Jeff during the past week.

He and his son had formed a tight, close bond over the years since Jen had walked out on them. So tight, in fact, that Reece had felt it important that the boy spend two weeks of his summer vacation at Camp Kimmiwun. Reece thought the time away would help to develop Jeff's sense of independence.

The parking lot was full, but he found a space and parked.

The first sign of trouble came when Reece was approached by a young counselor.

"Are you Mr. Newton?" the girl asked. "Jeff's dad?"

"Why, yes," Reece answered, wondering why he had been singled out from among the other parents who were also just arriving.

"The camp director would like for you to come to her office."

Anxiety twisted low in his gut. "Is Jeff okay?" he asked.

The teenage girl nodded. "Mrs. Walker's office is that way." She pointed along a path through the trees.

"Thanks."

Reece hurried down the path a hundred yards or so to the rustic-looking cabin that served as the camp office. He knocked on the screen door and then entered.

"Hey, Dad."

The fact that his son didn't get up from his chair and approach him was the second indication that trouble was afoot. Jeff was sitting along one wall, next to another boy who was holding a wadded cloth against his bloody nose.

Oh, no, Reece silently groaned. Jeff had been fighting. He wondered what the other child had done to incite his son's anger. Surely there was a good explanation.

"Mr. Newton."

Reece directed his gaze to the far side of the room where the camp director stood at the door of her inner office.

"Mrs. Walker," he greeted. Reece was very aware of the fact that the woman hadn't offered him a smile.

"Come in, please."

She beckoned him forward, making a clear and obvious point not to glance in Jeff's direction. The situation must be pretty serious.

"Jonathan," Mrs. Walker said to the boy with the bloody nose, "I've called the nurse. She's on her way."

Jonathan nodded, continuing to press the cloth against his face.

The inner office was small and utilitarian. Every inch of available space was used to its best advantage.

"Have a seat, Mr. Newton."

Reece sat down and watched the director round her desk, but she didn't sit down. Instead, she planted her flattened palms on the cardboard blotter and leaned toward him, her face a stern mask of disapproval.

Boy, he reasoned in his head, things must be *really* bad.

"We've had some problems with Jeff," she bluntly stated.

Reece gave the woman a moment to expound on her comment, and when she didn't, he said, "I've sort of gathered that." His lips pressed into a thin line. "Mrs. Walker, I want you to know that I don't approve of fighting. And although I don't know the specifics about Jeff's fight with that child out there—"

"Your son's problems have nothing whatsoever to do with fighting," the woman said.

"Oh."

"I wish it were that simple." She glanced out the small window and then back at Reece. "I've been the director of this camp for nearly fifteen years, Mr. Newton. Fighting is something I've seen many times before. Fighting, I'm comfortable with. I know how to handle it."

The tone of her voice became flatter with each sentence

she spoke, and Reece felt his dread grow heavier and heavier. What in the world had Jeff done? he wondered.

"Jeff had nothing to do with Jonathan's bloody nose," the director told him. "The child is just subject to nose-bleeds. It's his third this week."

Reece found himself nodding, but an impatience was brewing inside him. He wished the woman would get to the point of why he was sitting in this office, instead of enjoying Parents' Day with his son.

Almost as though reading his mind, Mrs. Walker said, "It's Parents' Day. And I really need to be at the opening session, so I feel I can't give you the time I would normally like to discuss Jeff's...problem."

His irritation got the best of him, and Reece frowned. "You keep mentioning this problem my son has. Will you tell me what he's done?"

The woman inhaled deeply, as if she was searching for just the right words to deliver the bad news.

"Mr. Newton, Jeff—" She stopped, straightened, glanced out the window and then looked back at him. "I'm afraid that he...has a problem."

"I think we've established that, Mrs. Walker," he said, impatience tingeing his voice as he pressed his back against the chair. "But how can I do anything to make it right, if I don't know what his problem is?"

Mrs. Walker seemed to steel herself. "Okay," she said. "Let me tell you about this morning's incident." The woman sat down in her chair. "Jeff and the rest of the children in his tribe were scheduled for an archery lesson. Your son disrupted the entire class when he told the counselor, Ms. Davis, that she couldn't possibly hit the target because...because her breasts were in the way."

The chuckle that erupted from Reece made the director

scowl deeply, and he immediately tried to cover his laughter with a polite cough.

"This is not funny, Mr. Newton."

"Of course it isn't. I apologize."

However, his expression of regret didn't seem to appease her much. And it might have to do with the fact that he was having trouble containing the smile that threatened to take charge of his mouth. Pressing his knuckles against his lips, Reece leaned his elbow on the armrest.

"I'd like to point out that Jeff did not use the term 'breasts,' nor did he use the word 'boobs.' The word he chose to use was crude, Mr. Newton. Crude." Her tone lowered as though she were afraid one of the campers might overhear what she was about to say. "He used the *t* word, Mr. Newton." She leaned forward. "The *t* word."

Reece kept his knuckles firmly against his mouth. The *t* word? His precious, innocent eight-year-old son had referred to the archery instructor's breasts with the *t* word? He didn't know whether to laugh or to be shocked.

Where in the world had Jeff come up with something like that? A hazy memory flitted around at the very edges of his mind. He tried to grasp it, but couldn't. Still, the elusive thought cast enough dark shadows that his smile faded.

"This isn't the first time something like this has happened," Mrs. Walker informed him sternly. "I've been dealing with your son's negative attitude toward the female counselors all week long."

Reece couldn't help but wonder what other offensive things his son had said or done.

"I do apologize," Reece said. "And I'll certainly apologize to each and every counselor. I'll talk to Jeff while

I'm here today. I'll tell him he needs to be on his best behavior this week. I'll make him understand—"

"Oh, but it's *you* who doesn't seem to understand."

The camp director pointed toward the door of her office, and Reece followed with his eyes. He saw his son's packed duffel bag sitting on the floor.

"Jeff is being asked to leave Camp Kimmiwun," Mrs. Walker continued. "You see, Ms. Davis was terribly upset by your son's comment. She was appalled, actually. She told me that if I didn't send Jeff home—today—then she would pack her things and quit on the spot. Mr. Newton, you must understand the position I'm in. There's an entire summer ahead of me, and I need my archery instructor."

A sudden compassion and concern softened the woman's muted blue gaze. "We've had other…incidents with Jeff this past week. None as bad as this, I admit, but…" She let the sentence trail, then she tilted her head as she went on, "Your son has a problem. He doesn't like women. He doesn't trust them."

She hesitated, her eyes darting away from him, as though she were deciding just how much of her thoughts to relate.

"Mr. Newton, I'd like to gently suggest that you get Jeff some…professional help. This attitude of his is not very likable."

How dare she suggest that his son wasn't likable! Anger welled up inside Reece like hot pokers, prodding him into action.

"Jeff is a great kid," he said, jolting to a stand. "A bright kid. And I won't sit here and allow you to indicate otherwise."

The sympathy in the woman's gaze dissolved in an instant. Her brows pulled together; her mouth became tight.

"You don't have to heed my advice—"

"You're damned right I don't!" The words burst from Reece's throat. "And if this is how you run this camp, kicking out little boys who make an innocent slip of the tongue—"

"Innocent slip of the tongue? You have no idea how obnoxious Jeff—"

"That's quite enough," he said, not even realizing how loud the argument had become. He stood, and with long, quick strides, Reece moved to the door. He snatched up his son's duffel bag.

He turned back to face Mrs. Walker, his fury still at a full, rolling boil. "I will expect a refund of fees for the coming week."

The woman jerked open her topmost desk drawer. "I have a refund check ready for you." She offered him a blue-toned slip of paper. "A *full* refund."

For an instant, Reece was taken aback. She was refunding his fees for the entire two weeks? She must really want to get rid of Jeff. For some reason, the idea only inflamed his anger further.

"Fine," he grated out. He stalked to her desk and snatched the check from her fingers.

The nurse who was squatting next to the child with the bloody nose looked up at him, curiosity lighting her gaze.

"Come on, Jeff," he said to his son. "We're leaving."

The child hesitated, glancing nervously toward the doorway of the camp director's inner office. Reece's fury turned to out-and-out rage. It was so clear that his son was frightened to move off of the seat without the express permission of Mrs. Walker. The woman must be a tyrant! he thought. And poor Jeff had been in her cold, cruel clutches for an entire week!

Guilt and a soft-hearted affection for his son mingled with the anger and insult he felt toward the camp director.

"It's okay, Jeff." His gentle tone drew his son's attention like a powerful magnet. Reece nodded and reached out his hand. "Come on, son. You don't have to stay here anymore."

Jeff approached his dad. And when his son's small, warm hand slid into his palm, Reece felt his heart expand and stretch, like an overfilled balloon.

The love he felt for this child was as sweet as heated maple syrup. Thick and heady. Reece savored the powerful and poignant emotions that being a father brought him, day in and day out.

And although the protective instinct in him was as fierce as that of the wildest, meanest predatory animal, the fury he was experiencing was calmed with one look from Jeff's innocent brown eyes.

He gave his son a gentle, reassuring smile. "Hey, buddy—" his soft tone was for Jeff's ears alone "—let's go home."

The sound of the front door opening had Maggie freezing where she stood in the upstairs hallway. The cold claws of fear gripped her gut in a tight fist. Reece had left this morning, and she didn't expect him back until after dinner, so who had—?

"Maggie?"

She exhaled at the familiar sound of Reece's voice, realizing that she hadn't experienced anxiety that sharp for days. She might be angry with Reece about what had happened the other night during the stakeout, but she had to admit that she felt safe with him. In fact, she hadn't felt this safe in ages.

"Maggie," he called again, "we're home."

We? Reece must not be alone.

"I'm up here," she said from the top of the stairs. Her curiosity had her quickly descending the steps.

She followed the short hallway that led to the kitchen. "I thought you—" She stopped in the kitchen doorway.

The boy looked to be about eight years old. With his deep mahogany eyes and coal black hair, he was the image of his father. The rummaging noises coming from the mud room just off the kitchen told Maggie where Reece was.

She smiled and lifted her hand in greeting. "Well, hello there. You must be Jeff."

Maggie expected his angelic face to lighten with a smile, but the boy didn't respond to her at all.

"Well," Reece said as he joined them, "I put away your sleeping bag, Jeff." He caught sight of Maggie and smiled. "Hi."

Jeff gazed up at his father. "Who's she?" he asked. "I thought you said we didn't need a woman around here."

Although there hadn't been a hint of scorn or malice in the child's tone, Maggie still felt insulted. The way he ignored her, it was almost as though he thought she was a nonentity. She couldn't help but feel that Reece's son's behavior was rude.

"We *don't* need a woman around here," Reece said. "Maggie is here because…well, because—" one shoulder lifted and then relaxed "—*she* needs *us*."

Maggie bristled at his statement; however, she remained silent. She may not like what he had to say, but she did have to admit there was truth in his tactless words.

Finally, she attracted Reece's attention with a forced smile. "So," she said, "are you going to introduce me to your son?"

"Oh. Sure." He looked down at the boy. "Maggie, this is Jeff. Jeff, this is Maggie Dunlap."

"Hi, Jeff," she said, trying again.

Maggie barely heard his mumbled reply.

"Why don't you go unpack your bag, Jeff?" Reece handed the duffel bag to his son.

Jeff took the bag and started toward the kitchen door. He hesitated, keeping his gaze directed at the floor. Then he darted past her, as though he thought she might have some communicable disease that he didn't want to catch. Again, Maggie felt insulted, although she got the distinct feeling that the child hadn't purposefully *meant* to offend her. The child's behavior was odd.

"You won't believe what happened."

Maggie turned her attention to Reece. She was struck by how handsome he was standing there. Even with the anger glittering in his deep brown gaze, here was a man who made women sit up and take notice.

Just the kind of man you should stay miles and miles away from, a tiny voice warned her.

Silently admonishing herself, she tried to focus on the words he'd already begun to say.

"...kicked him out," Reece said. "I just can't believe it."

"Kicked him out? Of camp, you mean?" she asked. "Why? What did they say he did?"

He shrugged. "It was nothing. He made some innocent little comment is all."

Maggie's brows raised. "An innocent comment?"

"Yeah." His chuckle held a strange, almost nervous quality. "He said something about the archery instructor's boobs getting in the way of her hitting the target."

Although she tried hard to control the totally natural shock and outrage that any woman would feel at hearing such a thing, Maggie felt it jolt through her nonetheless— like a sharp jab in the solar plexus. She crossed her arms and leaned her shoulder against the doorjamb. "Reece," she said quietly, "that's nothing to laugh about."

"I'm certain he didn't mean it to be funny. It was just a stupid, innocent little comment."

"I can't think of a single situation where such a comment would be appropriate."

He scowled. "Oh, come on. He's eight years old, for goodness' sake. He didn't even know what he was saying."

"Did you talk to him about it?"

"Well...no," he admitted. "He was feeling bad on the way home. I didn't want him to think this was *his* fault."

Maggie couldn't help but grimace. "But it *was* his fault."

"I told you," he said, his voice tight, "the poor kid didn't know what he was saying. He didn't understand."

"How do you know that if you didn't talk to him about this?"

Reece's exhalation was filled with exasperation, and he raked his fingers through his black hair.

Silence hung in the air between them, thick and tense. She felt badly for Reece. He was Jeff's father; he certainly didn't want to admit that the child was in the wrong. However, from where Maggie stood, Jeff's comment had been unacceptable. Intolerable. And furthermore, the boy needed to be told just that.

Her eyes were drawn to Reece as he slowly shook his head.

"That woman said that Jeff had a bad attitude—no, she said a *negative* attitude—about women. She actually suggested that my son needs professional help." He made a disgusted sound. "The high and mighty Mrs. Walker said my Jeff doesn't trust women." Then his voice lowered as he grumbled to himself, "Why would he want to trust a woman who was just waiting to toss him out of camp?"

Although she knew she'd probably regret it, Maggie simply couldn't keep silent. However, she'd have to tread lightly, she knew, because Reece wasn't going to want to hear what she was about to say.

"Well," she began softly, "if Jeff does have a problem, we surely know where he gets it from."

His eyes narrowed on her. "And what is that supposed to mean?"

She shrugged. "There are many clichés that fit—the apple doesn't fall far from the tree...a chip off the old block...like father, like son."

Reece stood there staring at her as if she'd grown two heads.

"Look," she rushed to say, "don't be angry. I didn't mean to insult you. I don't know if your son has a problem. I just met him."

There was more she felt needed to be said, but she bit her tongue.

"And?" he prodded.

He's reading you like a book, she thought.

"Nothing." She shrugged noncommittally.

"Go ahead. Spit it out. I'd love to hear what you have to say."

"Well..." She looked away, uncertain as to how to phrase her thought. Lifting her gaze to his, she tried a second time. "It's just that..." Again, she faltered. Finally, she took a deep breath and blurted, "Your son was pretty rude just a few minutes ago."

"To whom?" Reece asked. "You?"

"Yes, to me," she said, unable to hide her irritation. "And I think the fact that you didn't seem to notice his impolite behavior is...very telling."

"And just how was he impolite?" he asked, his temper rising. "When, during the sixty seconds you spent with my son, was he rude?"

"Don't be angry." She kept her voice quiet and steady. She didn't want to fight.

"Do I look angry?"

"Yes, actually. You do."

Reece tucked his hands under the opposite biceps and leaned against the kitchen counter. She could tell he was waiting for her to explain her comment about his ill-mannered child. And she wouldn't mind explaining, if only she didn't find the well-defined muscles of his arms so darned distracting.

After what seemed like an eternity, she was able to drag her eyes back to his face. "It's just that Jeff didn't acknowledge my greeting when I first walked in. He didn't talk to me at all." She shook her head. "It was almost as if, because I had *boobs*, I didn't exist for him."

She wondered if she'd gone too far.

"That's ridiculous." Reece's ire flared up like paper in fire. "What if…what if," he stammered, "what if he's afraid to talk to strangers? Huh? What about that? Every parent tells their kid not to talk to strangers."

She sighed, wishing he would calm down. But she knew that was impossible. He was Jeff's father.

"I'd buy that," she said softly, "if we were out on the street somewhere and you and I had never met. But you called my name when you came in. Twice." Absently, she reached up to tug at the short, curling lock of hair that lay behind her ear. "Jeff knew I was in the house. He had to assume I was an acquaintance of yours."

Reece pushed himself away from the counter. And it was so obvious that a thousand arguments were jamming his brain.

His mouth was a thin, angry line, and Maggie's guilt had her longing to reach out to him. She ached to smooth her fingers across his lips, to gently soothe away all the hurt and outrage he felt.

Are you crazy? the tiny voice in her head shouted. Why in the world would you want to get involved in Reece Newton's family problems? Especially after the way he attacked you the night of the stakeout.

Before she could ponder the silent questions echoing in her head, Reece took a step toward her.

"Let's get one thing straight," he said, his dark eyes granite hard. "I love Jeff."

Then suddenly, all his anger seemed to melt, and his shoulders sagged a fraction. He stared at Maggie, his gaze a mixture of bewilderment and worry.

"I love my son."

He walked out of the kitchen, and for a reason impossible to fathom, Maggie was left feeling horrible for what she'd said.

Why did she have to open her mouth and voice her opinion about Jeff? Why couldn't she have just let things be?

I love my son. Reece's parting words echoed in her head.

Of course he did, she silently reasoned. He was the boy's father. She could see the love Reece felt for Jeff in his eyes, in his face. She even heard it in the protective tone of his voice. And she realized suddenly that she found Reece's devotion to his son an extremely endearing quality. It was almost...sexy.

"Are you crazy?" she whispered aloud. This man questioned your judgment two nights ago. He blatantly insulted you. He ridiculed your professionalism in front of that jerk Buster—

He tried to apologize for that, a small voice reasoned, more than once. But you refused to listen.

"I was angry."

For two days? I'd call that being stubborn.

Maggie tried to ignore the tiny voice in her head.

You have to admit, the voice piped up one last time, Reece is kind of sexy.

"Oh, shut up," she muttered.

Chapter Six

"Are you certain this is what you want to do?"

Reece steered his car onto the driveway leading to Maggie's house and then shoved the gearstick into Park. She didn't speak; she simply got out of the car and glanced around the yard. Pushing open the door, he exited the car and then looked over at her, still waiting for her response.

"I had to come home, Reece," she said. "I couldn't put your son at risk. And that's just what I'd be doing if I continued to stay at your house."

She'd repeated the same words at least a dozen times, or at least it seemed so. The lazy summer sunshine beat down on him. Sunday should be a day spent sailing on the bay or picnicking by the water, a day for relaxation and forgetting one's worries. However, Reece felt his worries were just beginning.

He wanted Jeff to be safe, but he wanted Maggie to be safe, too. Unfortunately, the answers weren't simple. And since Maggie had insisted on his bringing her home, there really wasn't anything more to work out. The fact that she continued to refuse to talk with him, or even listen to him—about the night of the stakeout, about that heated kiss they'd shared or the fact that she was putting herself in danger by returning here—frustrated the hell out of him.

"I just feel," he said, "that there's so much between us, so much that needs to be discussed."

She was stonily silent as she moved to the rear of the car and waited for him to open the trunk.

"I just don't like the idea of you being here," he said.

Silence.

"All alone," he pointedly added as he turned the key to pop open the trunk lid. They reached in for her bags at the same time, their hands colliding in a tangle. She pulled back, her face stiff and unemotional as she waited.

"Damn it, Maggie! You don't even have a car. Yours will be in the shop for at least a week! What the hell do you plan to do...?"

She stopped him cold by closing her eyes and lifting one hand. Once he had her bags out of the trunk, she looked at him.

"I had to come home," she repeated quietly. "And I don't want to argue anymore."

Maggie reached for the luggage, and Reece balked. "I'm coming in," he told her. "I want to look around and make sure everything's okay."

"I'll be fine," she said.

But he heard the tremble in her voice. He'd noticed how her agitation grew with each mile they drove closer to her house. She didn't want to be here. He didn't want her to be here. This was the damnedest situation.

He frowned. "I said I'm coming in."

She pressed her lips together, but didn't argue with him.

They walked to the front door, Reece very aware of Maggie's growing watchfulness.

Her keys clattered together, and she slid one into the dead bolt. She pushed open the door, stepping inside.

Maggie's horrified gasp made Reece's heart thud in his chest.

"What the hell?" The swear escaped him unwittingly.

The living room was a wreck—chairs overturned, the couch cushions strewed about. The desk had been emptied of its contents, papers, receipts and envelopes tossed, hither and yon, on the floor. Maggie hadn't moved a muscle past her first step inside the house.

Reece let the bags drop from his grasp. "Stay right here," he instructed. "I'll look around."

"Damn it, Reece! I'm not some weak—"

"Maggie!" His voice was a grating whisper. "Don't argue with me."

Adrenaline surged through him as he stalked, alert and ready, down the hallway. Instinct told him the house was empty; the rooms, the air, just felt that way.

One by one, he checked each room, each closet, and finally, he returned to the living room.

"He's gone," he told Maggie. "Judging from the food dried on the counters in the kitchen, this mess wasn't made today."

Reece stopped suddenly, noticing how distressed Maggie appeared. Although she wasn't crying, she looked as though she was barely holding herself together. Her fingers shook, and the longer he watched her, the more he became aware of her trembling.

Keeping his tone as gentle as possible, he said, "It's okay. The house is empty. Whoever was here is gone."

He moved toward her. Her eyes were glazed over. Reaching out, he placed his fingers on her shoulder.

"Don't touch me!" She flinched and backed away. "I can take care of myself. I can protect myself. I can—"

"Maggie, stop." He kept his voice soft but firm. He forced her stiff body against his chest. Cold, stark fear emanated off her palpably. Her hands were clenched into tightly fisted balls. His heart nearly broke as she trembled violently in the protective circle of his arms.

Finally, she pressed her face into his shoulder, but she didn't cry.

"You're coming back home with me." He made the decision and the words were out of his mouth before he even realized it. "I won't let you stay here. Jeff will be fine, we'll all be safe as long as this…this *person* doesn't know where you are. If he can't find you, you'll be safe."

She mumbled what he assumed was the beginning of a protestation.

"No argument, Maggie," he said. "Let's go. We'll call the police—report this—from my house."

"No!" Her head snapped up. "No police, Reece."

"I know you said they didn't believe you before," he said. "But, Maggie, they won't be able to ignore this—"

For the first time since they entered the house, he saw her chin quiver, tears filling her eyes. "Reece—" her throat sounded raw and tight "—a policeman might have been responsible for this."

"I've been hired by Anthony Arnor's wife."

Reece's brows rose. "The county sheriff?"

Maggie nodded, then turned to stare out at the passing scenery. She hadn't meant to tell Reece about the investigation. She'd only just started delving into Arnor's background, and her research was in its first stages. She knew nothing yet about the sheriff's habits, or the places and people the man frequented. However, after seeing the condition of her home, after once again experiencing the overwhelming fear, Maggie decided that if she was putting Reece and his son in danger by staying with them, then Reece deserved to know everything regarding what he might be up against.

The whistle Reece expelled from his rounded lips told her he understood the magnitude of their problem.

"Sheriff Arnor's wife believes he's messing around?"

The probe had been gentle, but it was clear to Maggie that Reece wanted more information.

"Betty Arnor contacted me several weeks ago," Maggie said. "The woman had no information to provide, only some vague suspicions. She's chosen to remain in the house with Arnor until I've conducted my investigation and can give her some hard facts."

Maggie dug into her purse for a pair of sunglasses and slipped them onto her face. "I told Betty Arnor that it would take me a while to get to the case. I was working on helping Sally out...." Her voice trailed, then she rushed on, hoping Reece wouldn't interrupt. "It's nearly impossible to work on more than one investigation at a time. I only got the chance to do just a little preliminary work on the sheriff."

She looked over at Reece. "I'd spent so little time investigating Arnor that I felt it was impossible for him to have gotten wind of it. That's why I was so certain it was Buster who was terrorizing me. But Sheriff Arnor could lose lots of votes if word got out that he was having an affair."

The huge implications swooped down on her. Tension and fear took control of her with such unexpected and cataclysmic intensity that she felt she would surely lose her mind. Her fingers trembled. Her eyes welled with tears. The muscles in her face tightened, and she knew she was going to cry.

She hated feeling weak. She wasn't a weak woman! She wasn't. It was just that these psychological games being played on her were too much for anyone to bear.

Before she even realized what was happening, Reece had pulled the car into the parking lot of a small diner. He turned the engine off, and in one smooth motion, she found herself cradled against his rugged chest.

"It's going to be okay, Maggie," he crooned.

With her ear pressed against his shirtfront, she heard his words rumbling against his rib cage. It was a good sound. Solid. Powerful. Protective. Her inhalation was shaky, but she garnered enough strength from him that she was able to swallow her tears.

"You're not in this alone," he told her. "I'm here. Okay? I'm right here."

She sat there listening to the steady beating of his heart, and in just a few seconds, she was able to rein in her wayward emotions.

"I hate feeling like...like..." Maggie searched for the correct descriptive words.

"Like someone else has taken control of your life?" he supplied.

She nodded. "Exactly," she whispered.

The tactility in her fingertips heightened suddenly and the cotton fabric of his shirt became softer, the corded muscles beneath, harder, more defined. Some kind of electric energy began to snap and crackle like static on a stationless radio dial.

Maggie was reluctant to lift her head. Reluctant to lift her gaze to his. Even though she knew she'd have to soon. They couldn't sit here all day. She'd felt this intense atmosphere so many times before. It seemed to conjure itself, like some thick, unbreathable fog, every time they were alone together.

Memories of the hot, sultry kiss they had shared seeped into every crevice of her mind like warm brandy. Enticing. Intoxicating.

At last, she gathered her courage and lifted her chin. His mahogany eyes glittered with knowing. He felt the sensuousness that hung in the air between them, too. She read it in his gaze.

"Let's go inside," he said, indicating the roadside diner in front of the car. "We can have something cold to drink. We can relax. That's what you need right now...to relax."

She couldn't deny the gratitude and relief she felt that he hadn't commented on the energy that pulsed and throbbed in the car. "But what about Jeff?" she asked. "He's waiting on you."

"He's gone sailing with Derrick and Timmy. He's having a ball." Reece gave her a smile. "You worry too much. I think that's your biggest problem right now."

When he tilted his head to one side, it was obvious to Maggie that an idea had come to him.

"You know," he said, "you ought to take some time off. A few days, a week. Sheriff Arnor can wait. If he's the jerk who's been—"

He stopped abruptly, and she could see him fighting a sudden flare of anger.

After a moment, he began again. "If he's the one, then it just might be a good thing for you to lay low for a while. Let him think you've left town. If he's not the one, it won't hurt you to put off investigating the man's extramarital affair for a week or so. You need some space, Maggie," he told her. "You need some time away from this."

The idea seemed as sweet as vanilla ice cream melting on the tip of her tongue.

"That sounds wonderful," she said, and she heard the weariness in her own voice. Reece was right: she *did* need to put some space between herself and this problem.

Bright sunlight lit the interior of the diner, but the air was gloriously cool. Reece led the way to a booth in the back, and he signaled to a waitress as Maggie slid across the padded vinyl bench seat. He sat down across from her.

They both ordered soda, and the young woman went off to get their drinks.

Reece watched her closely. The atmosphere in the car had become quite claustrophobic for him. He'd held her in his arms, his only intention to soothe away the trouble and fear that had bubbled to the surface. But he'd wanted badly to trace her cheekbone with his fingertip, to smooth the pad of his thumb across her bottom lip.

However, it hadn't been the time. There was so much that needed to be discussed between them. Hell, he still owed the woman an apology. And the fact there was so much they needed to talk about somehow heightened the tension. But there would be time for apologies. Plenty of time to verbally review the kiss they had shared a couple of nights ago. There would be plenty of time now that she was returning home with him.

What he wanted to focus on now was putting out of her mind any bad thoughts, because he really did believe she needed to distance herself from her problems.

"You know, Maggie," he said, "I feel like I've spent so much time with you, yet I don't know anything at all about you."

The waitress stopped by the table only long enough to place the tall glasses of icy soda on the table along with a couple of napkins. Reece nodded his thanks, then turned his attentions back to Maggie.

"Tell me something about yourself," he urged. Then he asked the burning question, "How did you come to be a PI?"

He watched her gaze dip, and for a moment, he didn't think she would answer him. But then her green eyes lifted to his.

"I attended the academy—the police academy—in Washington, D.C., right after high school." She seemed to relax as she talked. "I worked on the street." She grinned. "On 'the beat,' it was called. I loved the work. I had a knack for going in and calming tense domestic-dispute situations."

She leaned her elbow on the corner of the table, and Reece took advantage of her momentary hesitation and let his eyes travel down the milky curve of her neck, her rounded shoulder.

"My superiors had me trained in counseling," she went on. "And soon, I found myself working full-time on women's affairs. Rapes, domestic abuse and disputes. It was tough...."

And frustrating, her expression seemed to add. Reece's heart went out to her.

"I mean, so many times when I worked in law enforcement, I felt like I was straddling a fence. You know, representing both the abused and the abuser." She grimaced. "Women often are pushed over the limit and end up breaking the law themselves. Or rather, they try to take the law into their own hands. And men who are accused of assault and battery are innocent until proven guilty."

Maggie took a long drink from her glass. "I felt the need to focus my attention. On the abused women, I mean. I thought that, maybe, if I could help them, get to them before they were pushed too far..." She sighed. "Anyway, I quit my job as a cop. And started doing PI work." Her shoulder lifted in a shrug. "That's it."

But her eyes darted away from him when she said those two tiny words, and Reece knew—or sensed—there was more to her story than what she was telling. More motivation behind her change in career. His curiosity refused to be quiet.

"You ever been married?"

"No."

Her answer was curt, almost cold, and it clearly told him that, whatever it was she was hiding, she had no intention of revealing it. Before he could delve further, she lifted her eyes to his.

"You weren't expecting Jeff home from camp so soon, were you?" she asked.

The sudden change in topic caught him off guard. "Why, no," he said. "I wasn't."

"Well..." She ran her finger through the condensation that had collected on the outside of her glass. "Were you planning anything special for the two of you? I don't want to get in the way of any plans you might have made."

"I hadn't made any plans," he told her. "In fact, I have to work." His eyes went wide. "I have to *work*," he repeated. "And Jeff's day-care arrangements don't start for a week." Reece raked his fingers through his hair. "How could my own kid slip my mind like that?"

"It's not your fault," Maggie said.

The gentleness of her tone drew his gaze to hers. She looked as though she wanted to reach out and touch his arm.

"It's mine," she went on. "You've gotten so wrapped up in my problems that you've lost sight of your own.

And for that, I apologize. Look, let me help you out. I'll be at the house anyway. Let me watch Jeff for you."

"I can't let you do that. Jeff's a rambunctious eight-year-old. He would run you ragged."

She smiled, and Reece felt his heart lurch in his chest.

"Hey, I'm pretty spry," she said. "I'll hold my own. Besides, if I watch Jeff, it'll be sort of a...payback. For all the help you've given me."

"Maggie—" his tone grew serious "—I don't need any payback from you. That's not why I've offered to help you." His eyes lit with a thought. "Hey, you said you'd been trained in counseling...."

She nodded.

"That camp director said Jeff needed help. Do you think that maybe, I mean, if you were to watch him this week, you could...?" Then he shook his head. "Never mind. It's too much to ask."

"Look, I see what you're getting at," she said. "I don't mind talking with Jeff. My training was specialized, though. Geared more toward abused women. But I have lots of common sense. And that should hold me in good stead against anything your son could throw at me." She tucked her bottom lip between her even white teeth. Then she said, "But there is something you could do to help."

"Anything."

Maggie studied him a moment. "I'd like for you to think about your son as objectively as possible. If he's got an attitude problem, then we're going to have to remain as unbiased as possible if we're going to succeed in adjusting it."

He nodded. The love he felt for his son was as big as the universe, too big for him to even try to describe. He only hoped he could do as Maggie asked and remain objective. Reece was about to thank her when something in her eyes stole his thoughts.

Abruptly, her gaze grew even more intense. "Why have you?"

Reece frowned in bewilderment.

Before he could question her, she elaborated, "Offered to help me, I mean? You said you didn't do it for any kind of payback."

She didn't look as if she believed that. Reece wrapped his fingers around the cool glass and hesitated. "Because I want to, that's why. I want to."

A small smile crept over her lips. It was the sort of smile that gave him the impression they had reached some kind of new understanding. Some new level in this relationship they found themselves in. He didn't know what it meant; he only knew he liked it.

Later that night, Maggie was in the basement of Reece's house where the washer and dryer were located. The laundry room was at one end of the basement, the other having been finished off into a cozy play area for Jeff.

Without having given the task much thought, Maggie had tossed Reece's and Jeff's clothes in with her own. No sense doing two small loads when one large one would cut down on time and energy. The soft, muted rotation of the dryer lulled her into a contemplative state as she folded the freshly laundered whites.

Dinner had been a quiet affair. Jeff had barely said two words. The acute silence only heightened Reece's tension where his son was concerned.

Her hand slowed its motion until it stilled completely.

Reece had worn this shirt. This soft fabric had covered his skin. Again and again.

Helplessly, she lifted the T-shirt and pressed it to her face. All she smelled was the light, clean fragrance of the dryer sheet she'd tossed in with the wet laundry. But she could easily imagine the warm male scent of him. All she had to do was close her eyes, which she did.

The sound of soft footfalls on the basement steps had her eyes flying open, her hands fluttering to fold the shirt, before Reece caught her. Her heart pounded. That was all she needed—to have Reece get a glimpse of her with her nose stuck in his clean undershirt!

By the time he'd reached the bottom of the steps and had rounded the corner, she'd tucked the shirt onto the pile of clean clothes that belonged to him, and she snatched up a white short-sleeved top that was hers.

"Maggie, can we talk?"

The hesitation and uncertainty in his question made her brows draw together.

"Sure," she said. She finished folding her shirt, laid it atop the small pile of clean clothes and then waited for him to continue.

Several silent seconds passed. Reece's gaze darted to the washer, and then to the clean clothes that Maggie was folding.

"You don't need to be doing our laundry," he said.

"It's okay," she assured him. "It was here, and I had to wash a few things, so..." She let the thought trail off.

He laced his fingers together, then unlaced them and stuffed his hands into the pockets of his trousers.

"Jeff's asleep." He rocked back on his heels. "Dinner was pretty awkward, huh?"

"A little," she agreed.

"My son completely ignored you," he said. "His behavior was pretty rude."

He looked at her for a long moment, his piercing gaze

doing crazy things to her blood pressure. Every warning system in her body jangled with alarm.

"Noticing is the best first step," she said, trying to keep her voice light.

She watched him take his hands out of his pockets and again lace his fingers together, his thumbs absently competing in a lazy wrestling match. He seemed nervous. So unlike the confident Reece that she'd come to know. Her heart went out to him, but she resisted the urge to actually reach out and touch him.

"I've been thinking *objectively* about my son and the problem he might have...."

Maggie's brow rose pointedly.

"The problem he *has*," he corrected. "Anyway, I've thought of some things you should know. His getting kicked out of camp hasn't been the first sign of trouble."

Her brow creased with concern.

"Jeff's had problems in school from day one," Reece went on. "Oh, the first year wasn't too bad, but second grade was a nightmare. When you forced me to really look at my son and how he behaves, I realized that his problems in school might stem from how he feels about women. I never put all the pieces together before. Objectively." He inhaled deeply. "And in order to think objectively about Jeff, I had to do the same about...myself."

The agonized expression that crossed his face tore at Maggie's soul.

"The idea scares the devil out of me," he went on, "to think that—" his eyes held a sudden intense anguish that actually took her breath away "—he's learned that behavior from *me*."

Aching inside at the pain he expressed, she couldn't resist reaching out to him. She slid her palm over his tightly fisted hands.

"I mean, I have friends who tell me all the time that I'm too hard on women, that I'm too suspicious, that my attitude is too...negative...too distrustful. My friends actually laugh at me. It's a big joke between us. But my son is *learning* from me, Maggie."

Emotion glistened in his dark eyes, and Maggie thought her heart was going split right in two.

"Why didn't I realize it before? Jeff is learning how to be an adult. From me. And that camp director said the same things about my son that my friends say about me. Why didn't I see it?" He shook his head in wonder. "And how the hell am I supposed to help Jeff...when *I* need help myself?"

Unable to resist the urge any longer, Maggie reached up and cupped his jaw. "I already told you I'd help Jeff. I'll talk to him, I promise. And I'll help you, too. Any way I can."

He looked so overwhelmed by her offer. Obviously, he had no idea how she could help him. Neither did she, for that matter. All she did know was that she wanted to.

His forehead wrinkled as his mind churned, and she longed to reach out and smooth her fingertips across his brow. Instead, she took her hand from his face and placed it gently on his shoulder.

"I came from a home broken by divorce," he began quietly, contemplatively. "I hated it, and decided very early on that, when I married, I would do everything in my power to make my wife happy. To be a good husband. A good father."

Maggie sensed that these words, these thoughts, were all new to him, as though he were working them out in his head for the first time as he spoke.

"I met Jen in college."

She felt him tense inadvertently when he mentioned his ex-wife's name.

"I gave her everything a woman could want. Everything. And for a while, our relationship was...okay." His breath left him in an exasperated rush. "Who am I kidding? My marriage was never even okay. It was awful. Jen was just so...dissatisfied. I tried to be a good husband. We bought a house. She hated to clean. She wanted to live in a small apartment. In the nearest big city."

He'd been gazing off over Maggie's shoulder, but now his eyes locked on to hers.

"I love this town," he said. "I didn't want to move to Richmond. I was sure that a baby would draw us closer together. Jen wanted a career. She said she would make a terrible mother, but finally, I talked her into trying. And she was dead right—she *is* a terrible mother."

Maggie felt the tension and anger stiffen his shoulders. "No wonder you're bitter," she said softly.

He looked at her, searched her gaze as though he would find some answers hidden there.

"I gave her everything, Maggie. Everything."

She massaged his shoulder, and then let her fingers slide to his biceps. "You gave her everything," she purposefully kept her tone whisper soft "except the freedom to *be*."

Maggie was relieved when his eyes lit with curiosity rather than anger.

"You both wanted different things," she went on. "I'm not a marriage counselor, but I think this is a pretty easy call. The two of you were just plain incompatible. And no matter what you would have done, what you would have given, I think that the only way you could have made her happy was to be unhappy—" she shrugged one shoulder a fraction "—living the life she wanted to live."

He remained quiet; however, it was so evident that his brain was absorbing her words like a dry sponge sucked up liquid.

"You probably view your marriage as a bad experience." She offered him a small smile. "But Jeff is a wonderful result of the time you spent with your ex-wife. You told me that your son is the center of your world. Any idiot can see that you love him."

Giving her a dubious look, he replied, "Yeah, but I'm teaching my son some awful stuff."

"Well," she said. "Like I've already said, recognizing the problem is half the battle. At least now you can do something..." She hesitated when she saw his eyes brighten. "Positive," she finished.

He nodded, rubbing his hand over his jaw. "You're right," he said. "What is that old saying...today is the first day of the rest of your life."

Now it was her turn to nod.

"I can do it," he told her.

Maggie had to smile when she heard the confidence returning to his voice. Reece was at his best when he was feeling in control. She understood that perfectly.

Then, his voice lowered, and his eyes intensified. "Will you allow me to apologize," he said, "about the other night?"

Chapter Seven

"Please, Maggie. Don't shut me out. I need you to listen to me."

He wanted to talk about the night of the stakeout. She had known this was coming. Had known they needed to talk. She hadn't been ready before now. She'd been too incensed by the way he'd jumped to such idiotic conclusions about her. About her work.

Who are you kidding? her brain railed. You've refused to talk about that night because you've been embarrassed by the passion this man stirred in you.

"Please, Maggie," he repeated.

He evidently took her silence as permission to continue, and she didn't stop him.

"I thought the worst of you, Maggie. I actually believed Buster—that low-life—when he said you'd talked his wife into leaving him." He pressed his lips together in self-censure. "Can you forgive me?" A smile hitched up one corner of his mouth. "I'm not sure I deserve it. But I can tell you that I've developed a new respect for what you do." His expression grew serious. "You help the women who hire you. When they can find help nowhere else. You put your heart and soul into your job."

His words melted away all the anger she'd been harboring against him for the past couple of days. Maggie was helpless against the grin that pulled at her lips. "You learned all that from one stakeout?"

He feigned insult. "I've only been on one stakeout, that's true. But the things you told me today in the diner— your motivation for becoming a PI—explained a lot about who you are. And what you stand for."

"Well..." She yielded with a shrug. He was complimenting her. Why was that so hard for her to accept?

The area at the rear of the basement in which they stood seemed to grow smaller. Then Maggie realized that was because Reece had moved closer to her. The look in his eyes intensified even more. His mysterious expression caused her heart to trip in her chest.

"There's something else that's been keeping me up nights."

There was a smoky quality in his voice, a sweltering sensuousness that heated her blood and started it churning through her veins, as fever inducing as hundred-year-old whiskey.

"Oh?"

"Mmm-hmm. You. And my memories of that kiss we shared."

He inched even closer—close enough that she felt his warm velvet breath brush across her cheek. A delicious shiver coursed down her spine, and she felt tiny gooseflesh rise along her arms.

Reece smelled so good. Warm and mysteriously delicious.

But wait! She wasn't looking to get involved here. And

she'd told him that the night of the stakeout. He, too, had said he wasn't interested in a relationship. That kiss had been a mistake. A mistake!

Without allowing herself to debate the issue, she took two big steps backward. Her thighs and buttocks came into direct contact with the dryer.

"Oh," he said, shaking his head, "I may have made a mistake that night—"

Dear Lord, she must have murmured her opinion aloud!

"And I've apologized for that. But you'll never get me to agree that that kiss was a mistake. Never."

His voice was silky sweet, like warm honey, and hearing it made her mouth go dry. Falling into his arms would be an easy thing to do.

Absently, she slid her tongue slowly along her bottom lip to moisten it. She watched his gaze become riveted to her mouth, and he followed the arduous trek of her tongue along her lip.

Desire, hot and thick, sparked in his dark eyes, making them twinkle and glisten in the dim light thrown by the low-wattage overhead bulb. He stepped toward her.

"Wait." She stopped him with one upraised palm, panic welling inside her. "We both said we weren't looking for a relationship. Didn't we both agree that we needed to…to ignore this…this—" she shook her head in frustration "—*whatever* this is?"

He continued forward, ignoring the barrier of her hand, until once again his face was scant inches from hers.

Her palm flat against his chest, she couldn't bring herself to look him in the eye, so she simply watched helplessly as her fingers spread themselves on his shirtfront. His heartbeat thudded against the sensitive indentation in the very center of her palm.

"I told you before, Maggie," he said, his tone a mere

whisper against her ear. "It's called attraction. In the most basic sense of the word. And it's foolish to ignore it. Foolish. I want you, Maggie. I want you bad."

"Oooh...but..." Her breathless protest was weak, even to her own ears. She wanted him, too. She wanted him bad.

"If I don't taste your lips, I'm going to go insane."

Maggie felt her heart slamming against her rib cage. And then Reece did the most extraordinary thing.

He smelled her.

With his nose pressed lightly against her hair, he inhaled slowly, deeply. And Maggie found the act so utterly sensual, so intimate, that her knees actually went weak. She pressed the small of her back against the clothes dryer and relaxed, only barely conscious of the warmth and slow, rhythmic vibration caused by the dryer's rotating drum.

"So, how about it, huh?" His question was husky with pent-up passion. "Let's just give in to this attraction. Let's just have one good make-out session right here, right now, and get this thing out of our systems."

Maggie hadn't heard a word he'd said—he could have been belting out the national anthem, for all she knew—because the whole while he'd been speaking, his hands had been caressing her upper arms, sliding along her back. His touch ignited a fierce hunger in her. Her splayed fingers curled, capturing a handful of his shirt in their grasp, and she tugged him closer to her. If she didn't feel his mouth on hers this instant, she would absolutely lose her mind.

"Let's just—"

"Shut up and kiss me," she murmured urgently, and reaching up to cradle his face between her hands, she brought his lips to hers.

* * *

Her mouth tasted wild and sweet, like juicy, sun-warmed peaches that had just been plucked from a tree branch. She tasted wilder, sweeter than she had in the sizzlingly erotic dreams that had plagued him in the darkest hours of the night, and his blood throbbed, hot and thick, through his veins.

Their first kiss had been an appealing appetizer. A delicious teaser that had sparked him to wonder, to dream of what was to come. Reece was ready for the main course.

Running his tongue lightly across the nectared surface of her mouth, he heard her moan softly. The sound was like liquid fuel added to the already-blazing desire that burned deep in his gut.

Reece slid his fingers along her graceful, milk white neck until his palm rested flat against her silken flesh and the curve of her jaw fit firmly in the vee between his thumb and index finger. Then, with deliberate slowness, he once again skimmed her lips with his tongue—and again, she moaned. Given the strategic location of his fingertips and palm, he savored the sexy vibrations emanating from deep in her throat. The sound of it, the feel of it, was enough to make him want to let out a groan of his own...but he repressed the reaction.

He leaned back to take a quick glance at her beautiful face. Her eyes were closed, her lashes fanning her fair, delicate skin. He knew her catlike green eyes could spit fire when she was angry; he'd seen it for himself. He'd also seen them grow gentle with deep concern. Helplessly now, he waited for her to open her eyes. He wanted to see her clear, green irises fill with desire—desire for him.

It only took one still second for her eyelids to raise.

The all-consuming passion reflected in her vivid gaze caused his breath to stick in his throat.

He barely had time to groan her name before he crushed his lips against hers. Her mouth parted, and Reece seized the opportunity to explore.

Her fingers wove themselves, none too gently, through his hair, and he pressed his body closer to hers. He slid his hand across her back, the fabric of her silk blouse gossamer soft against his fingertips.

The dance of their tongues held not a trace of shyness and only a shred of restraint. Having had only the barest taste of her before this moment, Reece had thought he'd surely go crazy from the deprivation and wanting. Now, as he was kissing the honey sweetness of her mouth, holding her soft, feminine body in his arms, he knew he was standing on the very precipice of madness. One step, and he could easily fall into the sensuous void that beckoned.

"Reece."

Her voice was a fervent, breathy whisper against his mouth as she tugged frantically at the material of his shirt. He looked down and marveled at the fact that she'd somehow managed to unfasten the buttons without his even realizing it.

"I want to see you. I need to touch you." Her voice was husky as she pulled the tails of his shirt from the waistband of his trousers. She didn't take the time to remove the shirt from his shoulders altogether; she only pushed the fabric aside.

Maggie's warm fingers trailed a fiery path down his chest, and when the soft pads of her fingertips swept over his nipples, his involuntary inhalation was short and sharp. He closed his eyes, relishing the feel of her touch as she curled her fingers and lightly dragged her nails across the shallow hills and valleys of his abdominal muscles. She hesitated when she reached the waistband of his pants, but then she switched direction, running her flattened palms around his middle to his back.

He looked down into her face, and she seemed happy that her touch pleased him. The small smile he gave her conveyed just how satisfying he found the feel of her skin against his.

Reece kissed her then, with as much control as he could muster. He kissed her mouth, her cheek, her jaw, her neck. And when he planted his lips on one particular spot just behind her ear, he was rewarded with her sweet, soft groan.

Planting his hands on either side of her ribs, he lifted her until she was sitting on the edge of the dryer. Instinctively, she spread her knees, her short denim skirt riding high on her thighs, and she hugged him to her.

The heat radiating from the very center of her femininity penetrated the fabric at the front of his trousers. The desire he felt already had him hard, but when she pulled him even closer, he thought he'd explode with the fierce wanting that surged through him.

As he kissed her lips, he worked the buttons of her blouse and finally he slipped the soft, filmy material from her body. The sight of so much pale skin was nearly his undoing. He noticed that her green gaze was intense, and her chest rose and fell as her breathing quickened. Her cream-colored bra was a lacy scrap of fabric that, with one quick twist of his fingers, was soon discarded.

Her breasts were luscious ivory mounds that fit in his palms as if they were made just for him. The weight of them felt good, felt right, in his hands, and he stared openly at her tightly budded nipples. Bending his head, he kissed the creamy flesh high on one breast and then looked up at Maggie's face.

Her eyes were closed, her head thrown back, her hands resting lightly on his shoulders. She looked filled with tension, yet at the same time she seemed completely relaxed in the throes of the passion he ignited in her. He was totally overwhelmed by the idea that he elicited this emotion from her. His touch, his kiss, was evoking this erotically sensuous response.

He trailed a fiery path of kisses from the swell of one breast to her shoulder, up along her neck and jaw, to her mouth. With one hand, he gently massaged her breast, while the other skidded down the satiny skin of her stomach, over the rougher texture of her denim skirt to the velvety flesh of her bare thigh.

She kissed him now, her lips searing hot against his forehead, his cheekbone, the corner of his mouth, seeming to urge him on. Mindless now in the desire that coursed deep within him, Reece inched his fingers higher and higher on her thigh, closer to that most secret place. And before he even realized what he was doing, he pushed aside the soft, heated satin of her panties and began a tender and loving exploration.

The mystery of her was hot and moist, and she murmured something unintelligible against his lips as their kisses grew even more fervent. She tipped up her chin, gasping, then she laced her fingers at the back of his neck, pulling him down and toward her. He lowered his head to take one delectable nipple into his mouth. He felt her passion building as he lavished her with sensuous attention. Her body quivered with mounting tension; all the while, the dryer beneath her exuded a slow, heated movement as the clothing inside churned around and around.

She was close now. Oh, so close to the edge. He could feel it in every strained muscle, in the way her breathing came in short, intense inhalations.

And at the very second she was swept away into the blazing oblivion, he lifted his head, intent on witnessing the sheer and utter joy expressed on her beautiful face.

After a few moments, the rising and falling of her chest slowed a little, and she took a deep, relaxed breath as she smiled at him.

"That was wonderful," she said, her tone raspy with spent passion.

She leaned forward, sliding off the corner of the dryer, and he helped her to balance until her feet were on the floor. Reaching around behind her, she snatched up her blouse, slipping her arms into it.

"Come on," she said.

When she looked up at him, the excitement that lit her gaze caused his heart to thump.

"Let's go upstairs." She took his hand. "I want to—"

"Wait," he said, standing his ground. "Let me just hold you a minute, okay?"

Maggie wanted to go upstairs, to either her bedroom or his, and make love. He read it in her expression, saw her intentions clearly in her sexy green eyes. And he wanted that, too. More than he'd ever wanted anything in his life.

She stepped into his arms, and he enfolded them around her, hugging her to him tightly. He wanted to enjoy every single second he had with her. Every single second.

He inhaled the warm scent of her and smiled when thoughts of fresh summer rain and dainty, brightly colored flowers came to mind. Anticipation pumped through him, inebriating in its intensity.

The gift she was about to give him would be wonderful. Special. An offering to be cherished like nothing else a woman could give a man.

He hesitated at the thought, a thin veil of shadowy apprehension dimming the intense desire inside him.

However, when she whispered, "Come on. Come up-stairs with me," he easily pushed aside the vague uneasiness.

Maggie preceded him on the steps that led to the first level of the house, and Reece had to grin as he watched her cute little derriere sway from side to side.

But suddenly, he was besieged with anxiety. What she was about to give him didn't belong to him. This gift belonged to the man with whom she would spend the rest of her life.

Oh, she might be leery of men at this moment in her life, but Reece had no doubt in his mind that, some day, some man would snap Maggie up and give her a lifetime of happiness.

So who the hell did Reece think he was to take something that didn't belong to him? If Maggie made love with him tonight, she would surely come to regret it. And for some strange reason, Reece abhorred the mere suggestion that she might resent the *closeness* they had shared.

Stepping up onto the first-floor landing, Maggie tugged on his hand until he was beside her in the hall. She turned and started for the next set of stairs that would take them to the bedrooms.

"Maggie, wait," he said.

The crooked smile that tilted her lips when she turned back to face him was blatantly sexy. An open invitation. "Yeah," she whispered, moving close. "I, too, need a kiss to tide me over till we get upstairs."

She reached up on the tips of her toes and pressed her mouth against his.

Her kiss was torture. He wanted desperately to forget his doubts. He wanted desperately to kiss her, to touch her, to tumble into bed with her until they were both spent and exhausted. But somewhere deep in the back of his mind, a tiny voice called for him to do the right thing.

"Maggie, wait," he said again, pulling away from her.

"What?" There was bewilderment in her gaze. "What's wrong?"

Reece inhaled deeply, steeling himself. "I don't think we should do this."

She chuckled at his hesitation, the sound of it rich and erotic. "Of course we should."

He shook his head. "I hadn't meant for this to go so far."

Her smile faded. "What do you mean? What are you saying?"

Reaching up, he began buttoning his shirt, his mind churning. Tread carefully here, he silently warned himself. You don't want to hurt her. Make certain to say something that will enable her to blame you rather than herself.

"I'm saying…that I don't want to do this."

Her eyes went wide, and she began to stammer. "But we have to. You made me… You didn't get to… I want to make sure you…"

She faltered, her cheeks tingeing with embarrassment, and Reece knew her sudden stiffness and discomposure was due to the fact that he'd brought her to climax. He hated to think that something so beautiful would cause her even a moment of awkward self-consciousness.

He let his arms drop to his sides. "Maggie, none of that matters."

"Maybe none of that matters to you," she said. "But it sure as hell matters to me. You'll have me feeling guilty because you made me…" Her face flamed when she realized what she was about to say. "Reece, you have to let me—" she hesitated long enough to swallow "—make love with you."

He rubbed his hands over his face. Damn, did he realize what he was giving up here? He looked at her, standing there braless, shadows of her tawny nipples showing through the diaphanous silk of her blouse. Of course he did. That was why the whole situation was so damned difficult. When he looked at her again, anger sparked in her eyes.

"Well, I refuse to stand here," she blurted, "like some high-school sophomore trying to talk some football jock into taking her virginity." With that, she turned on her heel, hurried down the short hall and up the staircase.

Reece stood there until he heard her bedroom door close. He raked his fingers through his hair, unable to believe what he'd just done.

Maggie flung herself onto the bed, her body pulsing and throbbing from Reece's touch, his kisses. With her eyes closed, she could still feel his fingers caressing her flesh. Still feel his mouth on her lips, her neck, her breasts.

Why had he refused to come upstairs with her? It just didn't make sense. Reece had brought her to orgasm, so in return, she felt the need to do the same for him.

Give-and-take. That's what making love was all about. Hadn't she learned that from living with Peter? Hadn't he drummed it into her head that a relationship was made up of equal parts of give-and-take? Equal parts.

Maggie had always felt that reasoning somehow squelched the spontaneity in their short-lived relationship, and in their lovemaking. But Peter had been adamant, and he'd been an excellent scorekeeper. Peter had never reached out to her, or anyone else, without knowing something was in it for himself.

But Reece wasn't Peter. He didn't act like Peter; he didn't think like Peter. Maggie sat up on the edge of the bed.

But was he really all that different?

She was grateful for Reece's help, his protection. And he hadn't seemed to want anything in return. Then she had offered to watch Jeff. Even more than that, she'd offered to try to counsel the boy. Maggie had felt comfortable with that give-and-take. It somehow made them... even.

But now Reece had refused to make love with her—after he'd pleasured her so. Did he plan to hold this over her head?

Heaven knew Peter took that very same tactic at the end of their relationship. Maggie still burned with the humiliation of how he'd made her feel.

That humiliation was what had prompted her to leave Peter. It's what had prompted her to steer clear of all women-using men. And from what she'd seen in her job, every male alive seemed to fit that category.

Well, Reece Newton might confuse the hell out of her, but she'd be damned if she allowed him to make her feel guilty or humiliated.

Monday morning Maggie awoke to find bright sunshine pouring through her bedroom window. She heard the television blaring and knew that Jeff must be awake. This was to be their first day together.

She padded to the bathroom, where she brushed her teeth and washed the sleep out of her eyes. After running the comb through her short locks, she went back to her room and pulled on a pair of shorts and a matching knit top. She reached for the door, then turned back to hunt under the bed for her canvas sneakers.

Again, she moved toward the door, and again, she turned her back on it.

How hard could this be? she wondered. Jeff is an eight-year-old kid. Not some mass murderer waiting to devour you. Chuckling at the thought, Maggie shrugged, pulled open the door and went out to meet the day's adventures.

"Hi," she called to Jeff, who barely glanced up at her.

The cartoon that had him mesmerized was some G.I. Joe type featuring shoot-'em-up violence.

"Has your dad left for work?" she asked over the blaring noise.

Jeff nodded silently, his eyes still glued to the screen.

"Hey, Jeff." She waited until the child finally looked at her. When he did, she said, "How about turning that off and we'll get some breakfast."

There was a moment of hesitation, and then Jeff reached up and snapped off the TV. He followed her into the kitchen.

"So, what'll you have?" she asked, pulling open cabinets. "There's cereal and milk. I see peanut butter and jelly. Or there's fresh fruit in the refrigerator."

"Can't you cook?"

She lifted one shoulder. "Sure, but why go to so much trouble so early in the day?"

Maggie stopped suddenly and turned to face him. Not wanting him to get the wrong impression, she said, "I *can* cook. I just choose not to in the morning, is all."

"Well, that's good to know," Jeff said wisely. "'Cause you'll never catch yourself a husband if you can't cook."

Whoa, she thought, tamping down the nettle his statement aroused, the fireworks have started early. "And what makes you think I'm out to catch myself a husband?"

"Isn't that what girls do?" Before she could answer, he went on, "My dad says that girls are always lookin' for the easy road."

Maggie wasn't even certain that Jeff knew what that meant. Oh, he had the pieces of the chauvinistic puzzle, all right, but there was something in his innocent face that told her he hadn't really put it all together. His tone and naive expression told her that he hadn't made the connection between "finding a husband" and a woman's "taking the easy road."

"Well," she said, "I'm not sure I agree with your dad." She turned and pulled a box from the cabinet. "How about some corn flakes?"

Jeff nodded his head.

"You grab the milk," she told him. "I'll get us a couple of bowls and spoons."

Soon they were sitting at the kitchen table spooning up crunchy flakes of cereal. "Like I said," Maggie went on, "I don't agree with your dad. Take me, for instance. I've never been married. I've worked to support myself all my life. I haven't needed a husband to survive."

Without a thought, Jeff blurted, "Just like my mom. She's got a career."

Maggie had thought to ease into the idea of counseling this child. She'd meant to take a couple of days to get to know him, and then broach the subject of women gently, gradually. However, here she was, deeply embroiled in a conversation that could very well blow up in her face.

She didn't want to talk about Jeff's mother. The woman shouldn't be blamed for wanting to live her own life, yet at the same time, Maggie didn't think she could ever find an excuse for a woman who completely abandoned her own child.

"I guess you're right," Maggie said slowly. "With regard to a career...I guess I am like your mom." Then, in an effort to put the emphasis back onto herself, she said, "Would you say that I've taken the easy road?"

One of his shoulders jerked up and down. "I guess not."

The next few moments were spent eating in silence. Jeff seemed to be mulling over what they'd talked about, and he seemed a little bewildered. Maggie hadn't meant to confuse the child; she'd only wanted to make him think. And it looked as though she'd succeeded. Counseling Jeff was going to be a snap.

Maggie was just scooping up the last corn flake floating in the milk in her bowl when Jeff reasoned aloud, "So, women either get married...or they get a job."

Where was this child from? she wondered. Mars? Did he not see the working women all around him? In the mall? The grocery store? On the nightly news broadcast? In school? Did he really believe these women didn't have husbands and families?

Then a simple idea struck her. "Jeff," she said, "what was your teacher's name?"

"Mrs. Johnson. Why?"

"Do you know what 'Mrs.' means?

"Well, sure," he said. "I'm not stupid."

She smiled gently. "I didn't think you were. 'Mrs.' means there's a 'Mr.,' right?"

Jeff nodded. "That's what it means."

"Did Mrs. Johnson ever talk about having any kids?"

His shoulder hopped up again. "Well, sure."

Maggie waved her hand in a sweeping gesture. "There you go. A career woman with a husband and family."

His brow furrowed deeply, and he shook his head. "But, Maggie, everybody knows that bein' a teacher isn't a *real* job. Gosh, they get the whole summer off. That's not working."

She ground her teeth together to keep from growling at the child, and she got up from the table and walked to the sink to keep from smacking a knot on his head. Counseling this kid was going to be a little harder than she'd first imagined.

Chapter Eight

Maggie walked along the shore of the bay, looking out on the calm, silvery water. She dreaded going back to the house. Oh, her days with Jeff were going as well as could be expected. Jeff continued to test her patience, but that wasn't the reason behind her dread. Reece was.

When he arrived home from work, the atmosphere became strained. Reece treated her with a bright friendliness that was so false it was sickening, and unable to help herself, she acted the same in return.

The thing that stood between them was as glaring as the noonday sunshine.

An orgasm.

Her orgasm.

And both of them thought about it each and every time they looked at one another. Well, at least she knew *she* thought about it. How could he not do the same?

"Maggie! Dinner's ready."

She looked up toward the house, where Reece was

cooking burgers and franks on the grill. Reluctantly, she directed her steps up through the yard.

Forcing herself to think on something other than Reece and the awkwardness between them, she focused her thoughts on her and Jeff's exploits of making potato salad earlier that afternoon. One corner of her mouth quirked up involuntarily. She'd wanted to prove to the child that she could indeed cook, and she felt it could only do him good to participate in the deed.

Jeff had been excited—at first. Peeling the skins from the potatoes with a paring knife was a new experience that held his attention. For about five minutes. He'd actually enjoyed chopping and measuring the other ingredients; however, he'd moaned and groaned all through the cleanup phase of the operation. But in the end, Maggie knew Jeff realized how much effort it took to prepare the food for a meal.

When she reached the deck, Reece said, "I sent Jeff in for plates and napkins."

"I'm sorry," she told him. "I should have been helping, instead of out there daydreaming."

"Nonsense," he said, his tone just a tiny decibel louder than normal. "You're supposed to be taking it easy."

"Yeah, well, it wouldn't hurt me to help out."

He had his back to her, his fingers flexing on the tongs as he plucked frankfurters off the grill. The very same fingers that had smoothed so silkily across her skin, across her breasts.

Stop! she silently raved. Just stop.

Her heart tripped an erratic beat, and all she could think about were the fantastic sensations that had coursed through her when she'd been in Reece's arms.

Please, stop torturing yourself.

Thankfully, Jeff came out onto the deck carrying three plates and several napkins.

"Didja tell Dad?" the boy asked her.

"Tell him what, hon?"

The tips of his ears tinged red when he heard the nickname. She certainly hadn't meant to embarrass him, and she warned herself not to get into the habit of using the affectionate endearment.

"You know," Jeff went on. "That I was enough to have Susan what's-her-name spinning in her grave."

Reece cast her a humorous look of curiosity.

"Susan B. Anthony," she told him.

"Ah," Reece commented, "I remember reading somewhere that she fought for women's rights."

"She fought for men's rights, too." Jeff's chest puffed out proudly at the thought of teaching his father something.

Reece's brows rose as he glanced at Maggie.

"Well, Jeff," Maggie said gently, "what I told you was that Susan Anthony wanted men to be granted their rights and nothing more, and women, their rights and nothing less." She looked at Reece. "That was sort of...her motto."

Reaching out to pat his son on the shoulder, Reece asked him, "And what was it that you did that had poor Susan spinning in her grave?"

Jeff's chin dipped, and he hemmed and hawed.

"He, ah," Maggie began, "didn't want to help clean up the kitchen after we'd dirtied every bowl in the house making potato salad."

"You made potato salad?" The question Reece directed at his son was overflowing with pleased surprise.

"He *helped* make the potato salad," Maggie corrected.

"Yeah," Jeff said, excitement lighting his brown eyes. "And it's awesome. Ya wanna taste it?"

"Sure, I do."

Maggie touched the boy on the forearm to keep him from darting from the table. She was pleased with herself when she didn't grumble as she stated, "Maybe we should stick to the topic here?"

"Oh, right," Reece said. "If you helped make the mess, Jeff, you should help clean it up."

"My point exactly," Maggie said.

"Well…" Jeff looked at his father with wide eyes. "I didn't think Maggie would mind if I went fishing. I slaved in that kitchen this afternoon," he went on candidly. "I deserved a little relaxation."

Reece's brow creased with a frown. "Don't tell me you left the mess for Maggie."

"Of course I didn't—"

Maggie could see that Jeff was avoiding her gaze, and the child looked worried now that he might get into trouble. She bet he was now sorry he'd even brought up the subject of Susan B. Anthony.

"I helped her wash every single bowl and spoon that we used."

Squelching a snicker, Maggie added, "Yeah, but only after I threatened to toss you into the bay."

Jeff seemed to shrink where he stood. He eyed his father, waiting to see if imminent punishment was coming his way.

Maggie caught Reece's gaze, and for the first time in days, the tension between them seemed to melt. They laughed, long and heartily. Finally, Jeff threw his hands into the air and joined them.

"Come on," Reece said. "Let's eat before everything gets cold."

The three of them sat down at the table and began passing buns and bowls of food.

"*You're* going to eat a *hot dog?*"

The stunned expression on Jeff's face nearly made Maggie laugh out loud again. But she forced herself to repress such a response. She could see this was opportunity for another small lesson in what had become, over the past two days, the child's reeducation where the female of the species was concerned.

"I certainly am going to have a hot dog," she said easily, forking up a juicy frankfurter and plunking it into a soft bun.

"But...but," Jeffrey proclaimed, "don't you know that they're full of *fat?* I've never in my whole entire life seen a woman eat a hot dog. On TV, ladies always stick to salads and diet soda. Everybody knows they need to keep a trim figure—" He stopped himself and eyed Maggie.

"Too late," she said, having made a habit of questioning each and every ridiculous generalization the child made.

At least he was catching himself now. And he'd also begun using the words *woman* and *ladies,* rather than calling all females *girls,* so Maggie felt they were making some progress anyway.

Maggie rolled her eyes at Reece, who sat at the opposite end of the table. She reached for the mustard.

"And tell me, Jeff," she said lightly, "why you think women need to keep a trim figure."

Jeff cut a glance at his father and saw he was going to get no help in that corner. "Well, ah, I guess...I don't know."

"You shouldn't believe everything you see on TV," she told him. Then she added, "You probably watch way too much TV, anyway." She'd decided early on not to emphasize his negative, chauvinistic attitude by telling him how dumb he sounded, but to rephrase his generalizations into more-positive words. "If women want to keep trim, it's because they want to live a healthier lifestyle, right?"

Jeff blinked once, twice. "Well...sure, Maggie."

"And it's okay if I eat a hot dog once in while, right?" she asked. "As long as I don't overdo it. But then, you and your dad don't want to overdo it eating fatty hot dogs, either, huh?"

Again, the child blinked, and Maggie could tell his brain was churning. Eventually, he said, "We sure don't. Do we, Dad?"

Reece was able to shake his head in answer, but Maggie saw that he was at a loss for words. She couldn't tell if that was a bad sign or a good one.

Well, she decided, he told me to do what I could about Jeff's attitude. And that's exactly what she was working on.

"Pass the onions, would you, please?" she asked Jeff.

The boy sat there motionless, staring at her.

She could see the unspoken questions in his eyes. She stifled the long-suffering sigh that her body, and her tried patience, yearned to exhale.

Maggie had no idea what the child's problem was now. But this was how her life had been since Monday; Jeff questioning every move she made, every word she spoke. He looked at her half the time as though he thought she was an idiot, and the other half the time as though she'd grown a third eye smack in the middle of her forehead. He couldn't figure her out; however, she was pleased that he was at least trying. If he was learning anything from Maggie, it was clear that Reece's son was slowly realizing that women were both a bewilderment and a wonder.

Well, it was high time Jeff came to understand what every other human male spent his entire life pondering!

"Jeff," she said patiently, "please pass the onions."

He looked at the container of diced onions and then back at her.

Suddenly, Maggie realized what he was thinking. How could she even *think* of eating anything so obnoxiously smelly when there were men present? his expression seemed to say. Didn't she know that, as a woman, she should keep her breath fresh and clean for the benefit of the regal males around her?

She stood up, reached across the table in the most unmannerly way possible and snatched up the small bowl of onions.

"Look, Jeff," she said, scooping up a spoonful of the smelly stuff, "you have onions on your hot dog, and your dad already ate one that was smothered in onions. Why should I suffer? Why should I be deprived?" She bit into the tiny piece of heaven and chewed. "I say we should all have onion breath together."

Jeff blinked, his gaze silently shouting, Someone save me from the raging lunatic!

Then the child looked at his father. "She's talkin' with her mouth full," he said, his tone brimming with amazement and disbelief.

Reece only shrugged.

A grin waged all-out war on her lips, and Maggie was barely able to cover her mouth with her napkin before it won.

After dinner, Jeff raced down to the bay to toss rocks into the calm, blue-green water while Reece and Maggie carried in the leftovers and cleaned up the mess.

As soon as Jeff left the immediate proximity, Maggie was besieged with that horrible awkwardness that had made her relationship with Reece so very difficult. The stiffness had seemed to dissipate completely during the meal, but now it was back, thicker than ever. Silently, they busied themselves, Maggie at the redwood table and Reece over near the grill.

The wall that separated them was completely and totally his fault, she decided. He shouldn't have—

Her face flamed at the mere thought of what had happened between them.

The orgasm. *Her orgasm.*

He shouldn't have done what he did to her. Reece had kissed her, hugged her, teased her, touched her, until her world had exploded and the stars had rained down on her in a million sensuous, glistening shards. But the worst part of it was, when she'd wanted to please him in return, when she'd taken his hand with every intention of leading him up to her bedroom, he had flat out rejected her. And in doing so, he'd totally blown the whole concept of give-and-take between a man and woman.

She'd been mortified at the time. And plagued with guilt ever since. She might have told herself she wouldn't feel guilty—but she did, damn it! She did.

She hadn't wanted to give in to this attraction they felt for one another in the first place. It had been her suggestion that they ignore the hunger they were feeling for each other. She had wanted to pretend it didn't exist. Certainly, as two grown adults, they should have been able to control themselves.

However, they hadn't controlled themselves. And now she was wondering why Reece had given...yet hadn't taken. This man completely confused her.

Maggie gathered up the cutlery and plates from the table, stacking them as neatly as possible, trying hard to push the erotic thoughts from her mind.

He'd given generously—the idea persisted—yet, he hadn't taken what she had offered. Herself. Her *physical* self, at least.

Again, she felt her cheeks grow warm and knew the heat suffusing her face had nothing to do with the summer sunshine beaming from the clear, cloudless sky. Maggie set the dirty dishes on the tray and made her way toward the door of the house. Inside, she began rinsing the dishes and loading them into the dishwasher.

Reece entered the kitchen, a bottle of catsup, the jar of dill pickles and a large container of mustard balanced in his hands. Automatically, she turned off the water spigot and went to help him. The open space of the kitchen seemed to constrict, and her eyes were helplessly drawn to his handsome face, his dark, intense gaze. She hated the fact that she wanted him so much, hated that she could so easily call to mind the delicious feel of his hands on her skin. She felt so *betrayed* by her body. She wanted desperately to conquer this frantic wanting that plagued her.

"Thanks," he said when she plucked the pickles from his grasp.

Reece moved to the refrigerator and opened the door. "I want to thank you." He placed the jar of mustard and the bottle of catsup on the shelf in the refrigerator and then turned to face her.

Maggie didn't move, didn't respond.

"You've been great with Jeff the last couple of days," he went on. "I want to thank you for your patience." He took the pickles from her and placed them in the refrigerator before he closed the door.

His hand reached up to rub across his jaw as he faced her once again. "I want you to know," he said quietly, "that I've been analyzing every word that comes out of my mouth at the office. I've been doing my damnedest to make certain I'm not condescending or...or—'' he grimaced ''—chauvinistic. I complimented Pam, my secretary, on the new dress she was wearing today, and I wondered afterward if my tone was in any way inappropriate.''

''Reece, I know that you want to change your attitudes and behaviors for Jeff,'' she said, ''and for yourself. But there is such a thing as going overboard. I mean, complimenting a woman on a new dress is a good thing. I don't know a woman alive who would resent a well-meaning and heartfelt compliment.''

He nodded, studying her as though he had something else on his mind.

Maggie pressed her lips together, refusing to say another word. She'd meant to encourage him, to let him know she realized what he was doing for his son. However, hearing how he was working to rectify his behavior only stirred her desire for him in this traitorous body of hers. And she was so afraid that the longer she stood here, the larger the chance that he would recognize what she was feeling. She feared that the craving churning inside her would reach out with invisible fingers and alert him to its presence.

After a moment of silence, he said, ''I just want you to know that I really appreciate what you're doing for Jeff. And for me.''

His voice was quiet, warm and rich, like hot, silken honey coating her skin, its caress absolute torture. He had moved toward her as he spoke, and Maggie realized that he was close enough now to reach out and touch her. For a moment, that's exactly what she thought he was going to do.

Please don't touch me, she begged silently. Please don't touch me.

If she felt the warmth of his skin on hers, she would lose every ounce of control she had. She felt trembly all of a sudden, and she tightened her grip on the stoneware plate she'd intended on stacking in the dishwasher.

She saw him raise his hand and reach toward her.

"Please." Maggie flinched back, hearing the blatant pleading in her tone. The embarrassment that rushed through her had her hurrying to the sink to load the last of the dishes into the machine.

When she finally looked up at him, she saw the last vestige of some dark emotion crossing his features.

Let him be angry, she thought. She hadn't meant to hurt him. She'd recoiled out of a pure, self-preserving instinct. If he misconstrued her behavior, she wasn't to blame.

Reece stepped toward the French doors that led outside, heaving a huge sigh, and the tension seemed to dissipate a little with the added space between them.

"I'll be out back," Reece told her. "I'm going to spend a little time with Jeff."

"That's a great idea," she said, striving to conjure that same artificial brightness they'd been using on one another. "And by the way, I want you to know that I think I've come up with an idea that's really going to wow Jeff. It's sure to change his mind about women—" she strained to grin "—and their place in society."

Reece's eyes lit with interest.

"Yes," she went on, "I don't want to give it away just yet. I have some reading to do, but I think that little boy out there's going to be impressed."

He slowly nodded his head. "Well, whatever it is, go for it. I trust you." With that, he ducked out the door.

When she was alone in the kitchen, Maggie glanced out the window. Reece joined his son, and together they skipped rocks on the smooth surface of the water. They laughed together, the image bringing a pang to her heart that she didn't understand. But then, there was a lot happening to her lately that she didn't understand.

She felt as though her emotions were in a turmoil. Reece Newton confused the heck out of her. He made her feel things, physical desires she didn't want to feel, emotional responses she couldn't comprehend.

Faint laughter drifted in on a light summer breeze, telling her that father and son had shared another funny thought or a joke. Reece shouted out, and she heard the two of them race around the yard together.

The Newton males were a rambunctious pair, and despite the awkwardness between herself and Reece, the loud and playful boisterousness that was a natural part of the tiny, close-knit family had kind of grown on her. As Maggie wiped her hands on the dish towel, she wondered if she'd ever get used to the silence of her own home when she was finally forced to return there. The thought was a dismal one, for in the isolation of her quiet house, there would be absolutely nothing to distract her from the memory of being in Reece's arms.

The swiftness with which the week passed was phenomenal to Maggie. She and Jeff spent their days with rods and reels at the shore, or cooking some new dish that never seemed to fail to impress Reece, or hiking along the water, or rowing a small boat in the bay. One day the temperature had soared and Maggie had impulsively jumped into the sunlit water; Jeff had quickly joined her. They had frolicked, and Maggie knew she'd never felt so carefree. There was something about this child that brought out in her a sense of fun and spontaneity she had never known she possessed.

Growing close to Reece's son was not something she had ever expected to happen; however, it had. Maggie found herself awaking with great anticipation to see those deep chestnut eyes of Jeff's shining with excitement over a new day just brimming with possible adventures.

This afternoon, the two of them sat at the picnic table preparing paper rubbings, a craft of sorts that involved covering a textured object, such as a shell or the bark of a tree, with tracing paper and "rubbing" a textured design with crayon, charcoal pencil or some other artist's medium.

Maggie watched Jeff concentrate on transferring the texture of a large piece of driftwood onto the paper. She smiled at how his tongue protruded from between his small lips.

She thought she was ready. She'd read all she could find on the subjects she wanted to discuss with Jeff. Certain that the information she was about to impart was enough to impress the most hardened chauvinist, Maggie placed her elbows on the table and leaned forward to speak.

"Jeff, did you know—" she worked hard to produce a tone of wonderment in her voice "—that there was a female artist by the name of Georgia O'Keeffe who painted such beautiful pictures that some of them are hanging in the Metropolitan Museum of Art in New York City?"

"Oh, yeah?"

He didn't sound very interested, and he certainly didn't sound impressed.

"And even though she was married," Maggie said, stressing the point, "she became famous in her own right."

Jeff looked up at her from the piece of wood. "She was married?"

"Yes, but she became the head of the art department of West Texas State University—"

"Who'd she marry?"

"His name was Alfred." Maggie downplayed this information. "He was a gallery owner, but the important thing is—"

"He was a what?"

"A gallery owner," she said. "You know, he owned the business that showed and sold paintings."

"His wife's paintings?"

Maggie lifted one shoulder. "I would guess so."

His little head bobbed up and down knowingly. "No wonder she got famous. She married the guy who sold her pictures."

Jeff's cavalier attitude miffed Maggie. "I'm sure Georgia O'Keeffe wouldn't appreciate having her paintings described as *pictures,* and I can't believe you think she *got famous* because of some man who happened to own an art gallery."

She sat up straight and tried to gather her wits about her. It hadn't been her intention to have a confrontation. She inhaled deeply, determined to try again.

"Have you ever heard of Marie Curie?"

"Nope." Jeff's attention was once again focused on the piece of tracing paper in front of him.

"Well, she was a famous scientist."

"Was she—?"

"Yes," Maggie said, anticipating his question, "she was married. Her husband was a scientist, too. They worked together. And they won a Nobel Prize in physics."

His chin tipped up and he eyed her. "He won a prize?"

"*They* won a Nobel Prize."

Her irritation flared when his expression told her that he was sure Madame Curie's husband had done all the work. However, she tamped down her annoyance. She would have liked a drumroll to precede what she was about to say.

"But," she said, pausing for emphasis, "she won a second Nobel Prize in chemistry all by herself after her husband died."

Jeff shrugged. "They musta felt sorry for her. I would, if her husband died."

Maggie's shoulders sagged, and she ground her teeth together to keep from saying something nasty to the child.

"They did *not* feel sorry for the woman," she finally said. "She made great strides in the medical field. Because of her, people with certain diseases can be treated with radium therapy."

The concept obviously went right over his head. This just was not working out the way Maggie had expected. Well, she had one more piece of ammunition to shoot his way. If this woman's achievements didn't wow him, nothing would.

"Did you know that there was a woman who fought in the Revolutionary War?" she asked.

"A lady soldier?"

"Yep." Maggie nodded. "She was known as Molly Pitcher, and she fought side by side with her husband." She thought it prudent to add that fact before he had the chance to ask.

"A woman soldier?" he repeated, his eyes lighting with interest. "Way back in the olden days?"

"That's right. And she was a cannon loader, and she

fought so bravely that, after one particular battle, she was presented to General Washington.''

"*George* Washington? The first president?"

"The very same one." She could barely contain her excitement over how engrossed Jeff had become in what she had to say. "And the story goes that ol' Molly was still bloody from the battle when she went to meet the general. The men praised her so highly that Washington made her a sergeant, right then and there."

"A lady sergeant back in the Revolutionary War?"

"You betcha."

"Wow, Maggie," Jeff said at last. "That's awesome."

She beamed. Then, when it looked as though Jeff was about to add something else, Maggie braced herself for one of his deflating comments.

His attention was completely focused on her as he said, "The next time Timmy comes over, would you mind tellin' him that story about Molly?"

Maggie blinked. That was it? she wondered. No disparaging words about Molly riding her husband's back to gain her place in history? Maybe her idea had worked after all.

Chapter Nine

Reece got out of his car, and the sound of laughter drew his steps around toward the back of the house. It was the end of the work week, and Fridays usually caught him feeling tired and just plain worn-out. Yet he found himself feeling invigorated and...alive. He'd experienced the same sensation returning home from work each evening. Somewhere between his house and the office, somewhere in the midst of late-afternoon traffic, he'd find his energy level rising in anticipation of seeing Jeff and Maggie together.

His son was always full of tales of his daily activities with Maggie. And with each passing day, Jeff seemed to grow closer and more fond of her. The change in the child was near-miraculous. His behavior toward her had gone from a grudging, reluctant acceptance to a familiar, almost devoted friendliness.

Standing at the corner of the house, Reece was able to watch Jeff and Maggie play their game of Wiffle ball without their knowing they were being observed. Maggie was up to bat. Jeff pitched the plastic ball. Maggie swung and missed. Jeff cheered. She tossed the ball back to him. He pitched the ball again, this time putting a discernible spin on it. Pride welled up in Reece, his shoulders squaring slightly, as he noticed his son's athletic ability. Maggie swung the narrow plastic bat, and whacked the ball far over Jeff's head. She yelped with carefree delight and then flew like the wind toward a round metal trash-can lid that had been evidently designated as first base.

The joyful, insouciant smile on her face mesmerized Reece. He had known that her time away from her PI business had been good for her; he'd seen the fear in her drain away. However, the strain that had developed between himself and Maggie had made it impossible for her to relax completely. A pang of guilt had him feeling the need to do something about the awkwardness that sprang up each and every time they were alone.

He was certain the tension was caused by the fact that she felt rejected by him. And all because he hadn't made love with her. He'd only meant to save her from doing something she'd later regret, but what he'd actually succeeded in doing was making her feel that he'd slapped her down.

Even though he still believed he'd done the right thing, he couldn't count the number of times he'd awakened in the night in a cold sweat, rock hard with wanting, his erotic dreams of her fogging his brain. In those moments, he was filled with regret that he hadn't made love to her; however, in the crystal-clear, logical light of day, he knew his original decision had been for the best.

He watched her run on toward second, her head thrown back as she laughed, and his body surged with hormones. He still wanted her just as much as ever. So was he really certain that giving up his chance to take her to bed had been the right choice?

Of course it had! She was a thinking, feeling human being. Taking advantage of her in a moment of weakness would have been wrong.

Reece rubbed his hand against his jaw. It had been an awfully long time since he'd taken a woman's feelings into consideration over and above his own wants and desires. An awfully long time...

"Dad!" Jeff was grinning as he raced toward Reece.

"Hey there, buddy," Reece called. "How are you today?"

"Great," the boy said. "Did you see Maggie wallop that ball?"

"I sure did." Reece glanced toward Maggie and saw that her carefree smile was gone. His spirits plummeted. He wished there was something he could do, something he could say.

Talking was the only answer, damn it! The only way they were going to clear the air.

"You feel like pizza for dinner?" he asked his son.

"Sure!" Jeff glanced over his shoulder. "Maggie, too?"

"Of course Maggie, too."

"Great," he said, turning. "Hey, Maggie, you wanna go out to the pizza place with me and Dad?"

Maggie hesitated, and for a moment, Reece was certain she'd decline. But finally she nodded her head.

"Okay," she said. "Thanks for inviting me."

Jeff fairly beamed when he turned back to Reece.

"Go in and wash up," Reece told his son. "I need a few minutes to talk with Maggie."

The boy scampered off into the house.

Reece saw Maggie's eyes reflect an emotion something

akin to panic, but she stifled it quickly. He walked toward her.

"I should get cleaned up," she said, her tone stiff and self-conscious, and she turned to the house.

"Maggie, wait. Can we talk?"

She lifted her eyes to his. This was not something she wanted to do. She didn't mind going to dinner with Reece; Jeff would be present to ease the thick wall of tension that she and Reece had built.

"Come on," he said quietly. "We're adults. Can't we just put everything aside and talk like adults?"

Maggie heaved a sigh. "Okay," she finally told him.

Without another word, Reece began to walk, and she followed. He unfastened the top button of his shirt. Inexorably, they were drawn to the water's edge.

"Sit down, Maggie," he offered, indicating the wooden bench that she and Jeff had used while fishing several times this week.

The feelings that slowly rolled inside her couldn't be described as nervousness or anxiety exactly; they were just plain awkward. And from the way Reece's eyes kept darting to her face and then averting, she could tell he was experiencing the same emotions.

"So, ah, how are things going with Jeff?" he asked.

"Just fine." And she had to smile. "I've got him thinking. And I'm happy about that."

Maggie went into detail about how she'd discussed with the child several women from history who were creative, intelligent and known for their contributions to society or their bravery during difficult circumstances. She named the women, told their stories. And then she expressed to Reece her exasperation when Jeff continued to try to credit each woman's success to the man she had chosen to marry.

"It was Molly Pitcher who actually impressed him." She grinned remembering the light that had shone in Jeff's eyes. "Finally." Then her smile widened. "Jeff became so wrapped up in Molly's adventures that he didn't even think to ask about her husband."

His mouth was cocked up on one side. "She was commissioned a sergeant in the army, huh?"

"Yep," Maggie said. Then, imitating Jeff, she added, "Way back in the olden days."

Reece chuckled.

"Of course," she went on, "she only received half pay. But she received it for life."

Huge, puffy cumulus clouds piled high in the late-afternoon sky. The sun felt warm on her skin; however, the heat from Reece's gaze burned her like a laser beam. Like a silent beacon that refused to be ignored, his eyes called to her.

She looked at him, absently tucking her bottom lip between her teeth. How could it be, she wondered, that she could feel claustrophobic here in the wide-open space? The broad expanse of Chesapeake Bay looming in front of them did nothing to quell the sensation of closeness she felt sitting here next to this man. The summery breeze seemed to die into nothingness, giving the atmosphere a profound sense of confinement and restriction. She had to work hard to suppress the urge to launch herself from the bench and race away from him.

Why did she feel this urgency to escape? she wondered. Was it Reece?

She studied him, his dark eyes glittering with a mysterious emotion she simply couldn't put a name to.

Or was it her?

Her heartbeat *ka-chunked* in her chest, and she self-consciously smoothed her tongue across her lips.

Reece sighed. "God, Maggie, you have been so great. There simply aren't words to express my thanks."

And then he did the most extraordinary thing—he leaned over and kissed her.

His mouth was warm and moist, his lips closed as he bestowed on her the most tender kiss imaginable. Reece's mouth touched hers for only the barest of moments, but it was long enough for her to feel shaken to the bones.

She blinked and gingerly reached up to touch her lips. "Why on earth did you do that?" The question slipped off her tongue like a satin nightgown sliding off silky shoulders.

"I'm...I'm not sure." His strong throat worked with a swallow. "I, ah, I wanted to thank you. It was impulsive, I know. I'm sorry."

Her brows drew together. He was apologizing. This man confused her so. He was tender. He was nice. He was like no other man she'd ever known. She found him so damned bewildering.

"Who am I kidding?" The words burst from him in a fit of frustration. "I kissed you because...well, because I wanted to try and smooth things over between us. The air gets so darned tight when we're together, I can't even breathe."

The honesty in his voice was so plain, so simple, it took her aback, and she felt the frustration emanating off him like invisible waves.

Now it was her turn to swallow. The frown on her forehead deepened as she admitted, "I know."

A graceful crane flew low over the water, its snowy wings long and delicate.

"Maggie," he said after a moment of quiet, "do you

think we could talk for once, without the barriers, without this wall of awkwardness we keep building? I want to know what's going on inside you.''

Keeping her eyes on the horizon, she tamped down the panic that threatened her like a huge, ugly sea monster rising from the depths. Reece had done so much for her. Offered her a place to stay when she'd had nowhere else to go. A strong shoulder when she'd needed it. Maggie had to admit that she'd needed it more than once, even though the independent woman in her didn't want to even entertain the idea. And he'd given her more than these things.... She pushed the sensuous memories aside, unwilling to face them at this moment.

And how had she repaid his generosity? By baby-sitting his son? How could she call spending time with Jeff any kind of payback when she had enjoyed herself so very much? Maybe not at first, but in the end the job had become an exciting adventure. So she really didn't feel she'd done enough. Yet Reece had never once made her feel that she'd shortchanged him in any way. He'd never once said one word that made her feel obligated or beholden to him.

Peter certainly had. That's why she'd finally left the man. She shoved the dark thoughts aside.

Reece Newton confused her; he caused overwhelming emotions and urges to well up within her that she didn't want to experience. And now he was asking her to reveal all that she was feeling.

Give-and-take. The idea marched through her mind like a chant. He'd given. He'd given a lot. Now it was her turn to give in return. And there was no better place to begin, she silently surmised, than the honest-to-God truth.

She swiveled on the bench so that she could look him square in the face. ''I can't figure you out.''

A spontaneous ghost of a smile gently curved one corner of his mouth. Maggie found it quite captivating.

"I take it you feel that's a bad thing," he said.

The teasing glint in his eyes made her insides go all
giddy, but she ignored the feeling, and rather than react
to it, she tipped one shoulder up. "I haven't been able to
figure that one out, either. Isn't it, though? A bad thing?
When you're around someone who always makes you feel
like your world is topsy-turvy?"

His tiny smile dissolved. "I don't know, Maggie. I
can't answer that." He cocked his head a fraction. "But
I can tell you that—" his brows rose "—I've been strug-
gling with the same questions."

She searched his gaze for only a second or two. He
looked to be in as much of a quandary as she. Maggie
looked out at the vast expanse of water. Pondering his
turmoil wasn't something she could do at the moment—
not when she was so preoccupied with her own.

"So—" Reece's silky voice called her attention
"—what is it about me that has you so baffled?"

In spite of herself, she smiled at the hint of flirtation in
his tone.

"I," she said, then hesitated a moment, wanting to get
the words right. "I guess I really haven't been able to
figure out just why you've helped me so much."

He frowned. "But I already told you. I did it because
I wanted to."

"I know that's what you said," she told him. "And it
was nice of you to say that. But everybody knows people
don't reach out to others unless there's something in it for
them."

Especially men, she silently added.

Several things happened at that moment. First, she got
the distinct impression that what she'd just espoused was

profound for some reason and that her words deserved a bit of reflection. However, the strange expression that crossed Reece's face caught her attention. She only had a brief moment to wonder what he was thinking before her brain was flooded with an overwhelming urge to explain herself further.

"Reece," she began, "I'm not an innocent where relationships are concerned. You see, I know what takes place between a man and a woman." Her cheeks tinged with embarrassment. She rushed on. "What I mean is, I'm trying to tell you that, like you, I have some...personal experience relationship-wise."

He didn't react to her statement at all; on the outside, however, an intense interest sparked in his dark eyes.

"I lived with a man for nearly a year," she told him. Maggie glanced downward at her hands. She sighed, aligning her thumbnails as she steeled herself to deal with her disturbing memories. "I learned a lot from Peter. I learned what a man expects from a woman. That love comes with a price. Everything is give-and-take."

She studied the knuckles of her fingers, and without realizing it, her verb tenses changed. "Every action had its price. Even the smallest favor turned into a loan that was certain to be called in."

Suddenly, Maggie felt swamped with terrible yet familiar emotions she'd thought she'd put to rest long ago, and they all centered around the humiliation and resentment of doing things for someone, not because you wanted to, but because that person felt he deserved it.

As she spoke, her voice took on a faraway quality that even she heard, but could do nothing about, so caught up was she in the past. "If Peter prepared my breakfast, I was expected to pack his lunch. He filled my car with gas, so I had to do his laundry for a week. If he took me out to dinner—'' The thought was cut off with a sharp, humorless laugh. "Well, let's just say that dessert was always served in the bedroom. God," she whispered, "sex turned out to be a nightmare."

Abruptly, she started, remembering that she was not alone but telling this story to Reece.

"I'm terribly sorry," she said, her face hot with disconcertion when she cast him a sidelong look. "I shouldn't be telling you this. It's just that I wanted you to know that I *do* have some experience with what normally happens between a man and a woman." She stopped long enough to moisten her lips. "I didn't mind the give-and-take. It's just that I didn't like the expectation that seemed to always hover over my head. It became very smothering. So smothering that I felt it would be best to live single and not worry about meeting anyone's demands."

She gave a quavery sigh. "You have given and given to me. You've provided me with a roof over my head. You saw to it that my car is being fixed. You've given me a shoulder to cry on, an ear to bend. Not to mention the wonderful emotions and physical sensations you..." She couldn't bring herself to say another word about what had happened between them in his laundry room. Maggie reached up and tugged at the short lock of hair behind her ear. "And all I gave in return was—" she lifted her eyes to his "—a week's worth of baby-sitting."

Reece shook his head as he murmured her name under his breath several times. The intimacy of his rich, whispery voice made her avert her eyes self-consciously.

"You know darned well," he said, "that what you've been doing this week is much more than mere baby-sitting. However, I did not—and I repeat, *did not*—offer you a place to stay so that you could spend the week watching Jeff. I *did not* call the garage about your car, or offer you a…a shoulder to cry on, so that you, in turn, would talk to my son about his attitude regarding women.''

He reached out and turned her to face him. ''Look at me, Maggie. When I told you before that I offered to help you because I want to, I meant it. I *wanted* to help you. I was not looking for anything, *anything* in return.''

His eyes were so intense, so open and honest, yet the confusion bombarding Maggie's brain made her feel suddenly agitated and nervous.

Men don't reach out to others unless there's something in it for themselves. The words rained down on her head like an unexpected summer squall. Those words formed an idea she'd embraced ever since her awful experience with Peter. However, since living in Reece's home, Maggie had found herself feeling perplexed by the fact that Reece didn't seem to fit the mold she made for men.

Could it be that she was living and thinking under the same kind of generalizations as Reece and his son? Only her generalizations were against men rather than women?

The questions were so startling that they threw her into a panic. But she'd had good reason behind the mottoes she lived by. She'd suffered long and hard at the hands of Peter. And she'd seen so many other women suffer, too.

''There's something between you and me, Maggie.…''

The mysteriously magnetic quality of his voice only served to increase the chaos that had taken over her thoughts. A part of her wanted desperately to focus on his face, on what he had to say, yet another part of her wanted to get up from this bench and run like hell.

''You can't deny it,'' he went on. ''And neither can I. Maggie, I was hoping that we could—that you and I—''

Full-fledged hysteria forced her to stop him with an upraised hand. She closed her eyes, fighting for some control.

"I can't talk about this right now," she told him, her tone corroded with anxiety and raw fear—fear of him, fear of the feelings he conjured in her, fear that the confusion that had invaded her brain would tempt her to do something she might regret. She needed time. Time to think.

"Maggie, I am not Peter."

She knew that. She did. However, memories of other men she'd dealt with hurtled at her like asteroids through freezing black space: Buster, who might not have run around with other women, but who had hit Sally just enough to "knock some sense into her"; the man who had betrayed his wife so often that she was just a shell of the woman she'd once been; the man who had spent his and his wife's life savings to satisfy his hidden cocaine habit; the man who had become so enraged that his wife had hired Maggie that he'd beat her into a coma.

"Maggie...tell me what's on your mind."

Reece said her name ever so softly, and when she looked at him, she noticed that her upraised hand was shaking.

"I need time, Reece. I just need some time."

She rose from the bench and raced toward the house.

"Hey, Dad..."

The serious tone of Jeff's voice made Reece glance up from the workbench where the two of them had sorted all the boards from the make-it-yourself birdhouse kit. A serious discussion was the last thing he'd expected on this beautiful, sunny Saturday afternoon. His son was holding a section of the birdhouse roof, but didn't make a move to place it on the bench.

"Is Maggie okay?"

Reece leveled his gaze on Jeff. "Sure, son. She's okay. Why do you ask?"

The boy shrugged. "I don't know. She didn't come to dinner with us last night and...well..."

"I told you last night," Reece said, keeping his tone light so as not to worry Jeff, "that she got a headache and decided not to go."

"Yeah, I know, but she's been awful quiet today. Is she sick or somethin'?"

Reece shook his head. "She's fine. She's just got a lot on her mind." That certainly wasn't a lie. After all the things she'd revealed to him yesterday, he knew she had a lot to think about. He'd seen it in her green gaze. But if she refused to talk, there really wasn't much he could do. Except feel worried and frustrated.

"I been thinkin'..." Jeff's voice faltered, and he averted his eyes toward the bay. "Do you think," he began again, "that it would be okay if I...if I like Maggie?"

The question surprised Reece. Hell, it did more than surprise him; it took him completely off guard. His brain seemed to short-circuit, and he had no idea how to respond. But Jeff stared at him, the question shadowing those big, innocent eyes of his.

Feeling a sudden fit of nerves, Reece placed the hammer on the workbench, looked at Jeff, then reached out and picked up the hammer. Finally, he absently ran his fingers through his hair, placed the hammer back on the bench and gazed at his son.

It was at times like these he wished parenting were a little more like a football game. He longed to call a time-out, rush to the sidelines and get some guidance and advice from the coach.

Reece would have loved to have the opportunity to talk

about Jeff's question with his friends Derrick and Jason. They would know what he should tell his son.

Yeah, a small voice intoned in his head, they would know what to tell him, all right. Derrick and Jason would advise you to tell Jeff that women were the best thing ever invented. Better even than...than the automatic transmission.

Derrick had Anna. And Jason had Katie. Both of his buddies were ecstatically happy with the women in their lives, so of course they would recommend a more positive answer to Jeff's question.

But, the voice went on, is that what you want your son to believe? That women are wonderful? Honest? Trustworthy?

Reece fought against the pessimistic thoughts. Isn't that the very attitude that had gotten Jeff into trouble at camp? Isn't that what got him thrown out of the place? And hadn't it been because of that kind of negativity that his son had experienced so much trouble in school? Reece had no other recourse but to answer the silent questions in the affirmative.

"Well, Jeffrey," he slowly and hesitantly began, "I think it's okay that you like Maggie." He shrugged one shoulder a fraction. "Maggie's a pretty likable person."

Jeff's expression held a huge measure of expectation, as though he wanted his dad to expound on the issue. However, Reece simply didn't know what else to say.

Finally, the boy said, "I know we don't need women messin' up our lives."

Reece's brows shot up.

"But Maggie is just..." Jeff scratched an itch on his cheek. "She's just like one of us guys."

The first part of his son's statement, the part about women messing up their lives, really needed to be addressed. Reece knew that Jeff truly believed this. Heck, Reece himself had believed it—

Now, why had that thought revealed itself in the past tense? Whatever the reason, he didn't have time to dwell on it, because the second part of Jeff's statement intrigued him too much.

"She's like one of us guys?" Reece asked. He thought of Maggie's soft skin, her flowery scent, her womanly curves. Hell, he couldn't think of one thing about her that wasn't distinctly feminine. He followed up the question with another. "How do you figure that, son?"

Jeff reached down to absently tug on one of his sagging crew socks. "Well, she laughs. Real loud. Usually girls just smile or chuckle. They never laugh."

Reece pressed his lips together to keep from smiling.

"And when me and Maggie went fishin', she baited her own hook. She didn't cringe or nothing."

"Or anything," Reece automatically corrected.

"Exactly." Jeff nodded, the grammatical revision going right over his head. "And there are other ways she's like us, too," he went on. "She talks with her mouth full. She can whack a Wiffle ball a mile. And she doesn't have all that long, tangly hair that gets in the way of her doin' stuff like—"

"Now, wait just a second." Reece stopped his son with an upraised hand. "Talking with food in your mouth is bad manners. Those rules don't change whether you're male or female. And there are some guys who have long hair," he argued. "I'm sure you've seen those rock stars on MTV."

"Oh...yeah." Jeff thought a moment. "Well, I was talkin' about normal guys—you know, like you and me. Maggie's a lot like us, so the way I figure it, it's okay to like her."

Reece pressed his fingers against his jaw, thinking. Maggie had worked so hard to impress his son with stories of famous, intelligent women from history. He wondered how she would feel if she ever found out that what turned Jeff's thinking around, what impressed the child, was not the fact that Marie Curie had dedicated her life to science, but that Maggie herself was "one of the guys," and could "whack a Wiffle ball a mile."

He didn't think Maggie would like it much, so he certainly wasn't going to go out of his way to tell her.

"Son, come over here and sit down." He led the boy to the picnic table and eased himself down on the bench. Once Jeff was seated beside him, Reece said, "Now, I want you to listen very closely to what I'm going to tell you." He inhaled deeply, and then gazed down at his son's face. "Maggie's a woman, Jeff. That fact isn't going to change whether she grows her hair long, or if she wears it short. It doesn't matter if she laughs really loud, or if she makes the mistake of talking while her mouth is full. She's a woman. A nice woman. A likable woman." The next words threatened to stick in his throat, but he forced himself to say them because they needed to be said. "Some women are. Nice and likable, I mean."

Jeff's small brow was knit with confusion, and Reece knew it was because the opinion he was voicing to his son contradicted the way he had lived his life and to the opinions he had expressed for a long time. Jeffrey's bewilderment was understandable, and Reece felt horribly guilty that this whole mess was his fault.

"Son, I know that I've said in the past that we don't need women messing up our lives," he told Jeff. "I know that I told you that the two of us can get along just fine. And we can." He reached out and touched his son's shoulder. "But I'm afraid that the things I've said—the things I've done in the past—might have tainted your view of women.''

"Tainted?" The frown of Jeffrey's brow deepened as he rolled this new word around on his tongue. "What's that?"

"It means, ah, 'corrupted.'" Reece tried to think of a more elementary term. "Poisoned."

"You poisoned me?"

"Not you," he explained patiently, a gentle smile tilting his lips. "Your *attitude*. About females."

Reece could clearly see that all this was incomprehensible garble to Jeff.

"Look," he said, trying again, "all the bad things I ever said about women were spoken when I was feeling very angry."

Jeff nodded knowingly. "With Mom," he provided.

His son's perception regarding the object of his anger had Reece feeling mildly surprised—surprised enough to hesitate a moment. At last, feeling the need to explain a little, he said, "Yes." He nodded. "It's awful, but I was angry at your mom. I wanted her to be—"

He stopped, remembering Maggie's words when she'd told him he hadn't given Jen what it was she had needed. The freedom to be…the freedom to be whatever it was that made her happy. Well, Jen had that now. Reece decided that he should be glad for her, not angry that his ex-wife couldn't be what he'd wanted her to be.

Reece shook his head. "It doesn't matter what I wanted. I expected too much from your mom. A person can only give what they're able to give, right?"

"Right."

"And your mom gives what she can," he went on. "And I was wrong to be angry. I was wrong to say things against her. And I was wrong to allow my anger to rub off on you."

It broke Reece's heart to see his son trying so very hard to comprehend what he was being told. However, it was evident that this subject was too complicated, this problem too complex, for Jeff to grasp.

"It's okay if you don't understand," Reece said. "We'll work on it, okay? We'll talk about it some more. We don't have to solve everything today."

Jeff nodded, looking a little relieved.

Reece chuckled and ruffled his son's dark hair. "What I do want you to understand—" he looked at his son with the most serious expression "—is that women are people. Just like you and me. They deserve your respect. They're honorable and trustworthy. You should appreciate and be courteous to any women you come into contact with. Mothers of your friends. Teachers. Camp counselors."

He looked at Jeff pointedly, and Jeff blinked, his shoulders slumping.

"Now, I'm not scolding you," Reece assured him. "I'm talking to you, man-to-man." He grinned. "I'm learning all these things myself. And I'm learning them because, well, because Maggie helped me to understand."

Reece was filled with a sudden awe as he realized just how much Maggie had changed his life in the short time he'd known her.

Patting his son's shoulder lightly, he said, "It's okay to like Maggie." His grin widened a fraction. "I kinda like her myself. Now, let's go over there and make that birdhouse."

As he went across the yard with Jeff, Reece couldn't help but ponder all the things he'd said about women in general. And about Maggie specifically. The woman *had* changed his life. That was an undeniable fact. She'd forced him to look at himself and his attitudes the way no one else had. Maggie had made him question and re-think his viewpoint on females from day one. And the attraction he'd felt toward her from the very beginning was utterly phenomenal.

The sweet taste of her honeyed lips, the feel of her heated, velvet-soft skin, the sight of her ecstasy-filled expression when he'd taken her to the heights of desire—these memories had continued to haunt him ever since the passionate moments he'd spent holding her in his arms, yet they were memories he wouldn't give up for the world.

That night had caused a strain between them, but it was a night he'd never forget. She was angry that he hadn't taken her to bed, and after all that she'd told him about that jerk Peter, Reece understood now better than ever what Maggie had been feeling. She'd presumed he would expect some kind of payback for the fact that he'd brought her to orgasm.

The very idea was strange. Almost twisted. However, that's how Maggie believed things should be. And it was no wonder after what she'd been through. However, Reece could only tell her that he didn't expect anything from her. He couldn't make her believe it. That was a conclusion she had to come to on her own.

And yes, he might regret the fact that he hadn't taken her to bed; however, he still believed he'd done the right thing. Before consummating a relationship, two people needed to commit themselves to...

To what? he wondered. To the future. To each other. Reece gave a mental shrug. He wasn't certain.

Reece told his son that he *liked* Maggie, but after talking with her down by the bay yesterday, Reece was left wondering just how much of a gross understatement that confession might have been....

Chapter Ten

Reece plucked a piece of popcorn from the bowl and popped it into his mouth. Even though the old black-and-white movie blaring from the TV was in its most-climactic moments—the Sioux war party had the wagon train surrounded, and the settlers wondered if the cavalry would arrive in time to save them—Reece was having a terrible time concentrating on the film. He looked down at Jeff sitting beside him. His son was unblinkingly enthralled with the exciting images of the American Old West depicted on the television screen.

Absently, Reece savored the salty taste of the kernel of popcorn before he bit down and chewed, unbidden thoughts of Maggie once again intruding on his mind.

What was she doing up there in her room? he wondered. She'd seemed antsy and nervous all weekend, and he knew she was dealing with some dark memories of the jerk who had mistreated her.

Reece hoped that she would come to believe in him, that she would finally be convinced he was nothing like the man she'd lived with, that he was nothing like any of the men she'd come into contact with in her line of work. Until she came to that realization, their relationship was at a stalemate.

Seeing movement in the periphery of his vision, he looked up and saw her enter the room. And as always, the sight of her was like a swift kick in the gut. She looked so damned good.

"Hi, Maggie," Jeff said.

She smiled at him in greeting, but Reece could see the lines of stress around her mouth. Maggie's eyes darted toward him, and Reece felt the tension and awkwardness snap and spark in the air.

He tossed her a small grin filled with a self-assuredness that was purely false, hoping the friendly overture would delete some of the stiffness between them. She only averted her gaze to the floor. How he had hoped to dissolve the barrier, but it was there just as strong as ever.

She wore dark, clingy trouser things…leggings, he thought. The knit fabric looked cottony soft, and it hugged her form provocatively. The top she wore was a deep maroon that emphasized her creamy, smooth skin and flaming red hair. She looked so sexy his mouth went dry.

Just then, the TV emitted a cacophony of sound as the cavalry in the movie crested the hill, the trumpet player blasting the issue to charge.

"This is the best part," Jeff exclaimed. "Can you watch it with us, Maggie?"

Reece watched her closely as she looked at his son; a fond smile tugged and then lingered at one corner of her mouth. He found it quite captivating, and the urge to kiss her lips welled up inside him with a startling strength.

"Sure," she told Jeffrey, and she rounded the coffee

table and sat on the couch so that the boy was positioned between herself and Reece.

The soft, feminine scent of her wafted around him like the smell of raindrops and honeysuckle. Reece inhaled it deeply into his lungs. He longed to look at her. So much so that he had a difficult time keeping his eyes on the TV screen.

Finally, the impulse to cast a quick glance her way became unbearable, and Reece caved in to it. He met her gaze head-on, and he felt his cheeks grow warm with chagrin; however, he didn't avert his eyes, but stared at her steadily. The shadows that filled her green gaze worried him, and he frowned.

"Can we talk?" she asked, her tone whisper soft. "I mean...a little later?"

"Shh." Jeff pressed his index finger to his lips. "The good guys are comin' to the rescue. We're gonna miss the best part."

Reece nodded to Maggie over his son's head as he felt his heart race. What was it she wanted to discuss? he wondered. Could it be she'd thought out her feelings and was ready to reveal them to him? Barely aware of the action-packed conclusion to the movie, Reece's mind churned with questions.

"Aw, gross!"

Jeff's outburst made Reece blink and look at the television, where he saw the hero and heroine of the film in a final, tender embrace. Maggie chuckled softly, and Reece joined her as the closing credits began to roll.

"Okay, pal," Reece said to his son, "it's bedtime."

"Aw, Dad, can't I just stay up—?"

"No way," he interrupted. "Up to bed."

Jeff grumbled as he slid off the couch and padded toward the doorway.

"Don't forget to brush your teeth," Reece reminded him. "I'll be up in a few minutes to tuck you in."

Before Jeff disappeared from sight, Maggie quietly called, "Night, Jeff."

The boy paused and gave Maggie a miserable look. "Good night, Maggie," he said, and he was gone.

When they were alone, Reece turned to Maggie. He was surprised to see that she was grinning.

"Your son—" her smile widened "—is something else."

She actually chuckled. The silky sound caused the hairs on the back of his neck to rise. Lord, but she was beautiful.

"Remember when I first came?" she went on. "How he ignored me?" She glanced toward the empty doorway. "Yep, Jeff's gonna be all right."

"Because of you," he commented.

Maggie's smile was benign, yet he could see a storm brewing in her gaze. He wanted to take her hand, to tell her all the things he was feeling, but he knew she needed to be the one who brought up the subject of their relationship. "So, what did you want to talk about?"

Her green gaze lowered for a second and then rose again to his face. Finally, she said, "I need to know when my car will be ready."

The subject she chose caught him off guard. "Well, the garage said it'd be ready the first of the week. I took that to mean Monday or Tuesday. I'll call first thing tomorrow."

She nodded. "I need to get back to work. It's been great to take some time off, but I'll never solve this thing hanging over me until I get pictures of the sheriff and hand them over to his wife. Once that's done, he'll have no more reason to be concerned with me."

"*Concerned* with you?" He couldn't keep the incredulity from his tone. "Aren't you describing the man's behavior rather mildly?"

"Look, Reece," she said, "I have a job to do. I have to get back to it. I have bills to pay. Responsibilities to meet. A life to live. I won't allow this man to keep me from it any longer." She ran her fingers through her short red hair. "I just wanted to know when my car would be ready."

Maggie stood up to leave, and Reece felt his brow crease deeply.

But…but, he wanted to say, *isn't there something else you wanted to talk about? What about us, damn it? What about us?*

His questions showed clearly in his eyes; he knew it. Could feel it. And at least Maggie had sense enough to look uncomfortable.

Her tongue darted out to moisten her bottom lip, and she shook her head slowly. "I'm just not ready," she whispered. Then she turned and walked out of the room.

He wanted to chase after her. Hound her until she told him everything that was going through her head. Everything that she was feeling, whether it be good or bad, positive or negative. But he had to let her go. He had to.

He had to let her find her own way. She'd said she wasn't ready. Reece knew he had to wait until she was. He had to allow her the freedom to be….

Even if it killed him.

"Is she certain she's got the right guy?"

Derrick's face expressed his shock as he asked Reece the question.

Reece could only nod. "Maggie seems to think so."

Jason just sat there, a dark and dubious look in his eyes.

It was Tuesday night, and Reece had called a special meeting of the Single Daddy Club. Today had been filled with one hellish experience after another, and it had all started early when Joey, the claims adjuster who had first introduced him to Maggie, had been called home due to a death in the family. Reece felt terrible about the young man's plight. Then, due to the staff shortage, the office had been swamped with work. He'd arrived home only to find a note from Maggie saying that her car had been delivered and that she had gone out "on the hunt," as she had put it. He'd worried himself sick for two solid hours, pacing around the house, thoughts of her tailing a maniac rolling through his head. But he had to allow her the freedom to be, he kept telling himself. He simply had to.

Finally, he'd picked up the telephone and called Jason and Derrick. Now the three men sat around Reece's kitchen table sharing a little time and a couple of beers together. Reece was certain that, with his friends here with him, he could get through the evening without completely losing his mind.

He probably shouldn't have told them about Maggie's investigation of Sheriff Anthony Arnor, but he'd asked them to keep the information confidential. Besides, he really needed the support of his friends right now.

Jason finally spoke up. "Reece, I know Sheriff Arnor. He isn't the kind of man who would fool around on his wife…and I just can't see him breaking into someone's home, playing terrifying mind games. I just can't believe it. Are you sure she's got the right man?"

"Of course, there's no way she can be positive," Reece said. "Not without catching the bastard in the act."

"Could it be—" Jason leaned an elbow on the edge of the table "—someone she's investigated in the past?"

"It's possible. Although Maggie seems to think that once a case is closed, there's no reason for anyone to try to thwart her efforts."

Derrick smoothed his fingertips over the damp surface of his half-filled beer bottle. "In her line of work," he softly stated, "she must have angered a lot of people."

"Revenge is a great motivator," Jason agreed.

The idea struck Reece with enough force to take his breath away. "My God, it could be any one of the men she's dug up dirt on."

"Or their wives or girlfriends..."

Jason's comment elicited a perplexed look from Reece.

"Women are notorious for changing their minds. If a woman decides she wants to stay with her husband—despite the information Maggie has shoved in her face—who is she going to blame? The loving man in her life?" Jason's short, sharp laugh was humorless. "I doubt that."

Reece swore under his breath. "Do you realize that the list of suspects just doubled?" He looked at Jason. "How well do you know Arnor? Are you sure it *couldn't* be him?"

"I'm not sure, no," Jason said. "But all my years as a police officer are telling me that Maggie's trying to catch the wrong tiger."

"Look—" Derrick left his beer untouched as he leaned toward Reece "—do you have access to any information about Maggie's past cases?"

Tapping a knuckle against his chin, Reece took a moment to think. "She brought a huge briefcase with her when she came. I think she was afraid the jerk would get into her house and destroy her records. I haven't seen the briefcase since she came, but I would assume it's still upstairs."

His friends made to rise.

"Wait, guys. Now, just hold on." Reece had planted his hands on the tabletop. "I can't go invading Maggie's privacy like this. I trust her ability. She's good at what she does. I need to give her the space she needs to make her own way. I don't want her to think I'm intruding. And besides, she's got a lot on her mind right now. You see, we've...she's..." The fact that he'd begun to stammer caught his attention, and he snapped his jaw shut.

Both Jason and Derrick sat there at the table, staring and speechless. Reece felt his face grow warm. He reached up to rub his jaw in an attempt to cover his embarrassment. An acute silence hung heavy among the three of them, and Reece realized that, as friends, they had never experienced this kind of discomfort when they were together.

"Gee, Reece," Jason said, looking perplexed, "you're talking about trust, you're complimenting Maggie, saying that she needs to be treated with respect and common courtesy." His brows rose. "Is there something you want to tell us about Maggie?"

A ragged sigh escaped Reece's throat. "I haven't figured it all out myself." He heard the self-consciousness in his tone.

"Oh, I dunno," Derrick commented, a devilish gleam lighting his gaze. "I think you've figured it out, Reece. And if the situation wasn't so darned serious, I'd be teasing the hell out of you...lover boy."

Reece grimaced, and then narrowed his eyes on Derrick. "Don't start."

Derrick only grinned.

"Look, Reece," Jason said, "I understand your wanting to give Maggie some space. Especially if she's thinking over some matters of the heart."

Reece knew Jason was choosing his words carefully and he appreciated that.

"But, like Derrick pointed out, this situation is serious." He leaned back and crossed his arms over his chest. "If Maggie's right and Arnor is the guy she's looking for, then she should have some kind of backup. The behavior you described regarding the person breaking into Maggie's home is twisted. This isn't a rational human being we're talking about." Jason shifted in his chair. "If Arnor is innocent, then that means there's someone out there...someone who has it in for Maggie. And if this joker was stalking her at her home, the next logical step would be for him to go out looking for her. Especially if he's frustrated that she moved out of her house and he can no longer terrorize her there."

Anxiety, thick and sweaty, crept up on Reece. "But we haven't had even a hint that this person knows she's here. As long as he doesn't know where she is..." Seeing Jason shake his head, Reece let the rest of the sentence fade.

"You had her car worked on," Jason said. "Anyone working at the garage could give her away. They have no idea her whereabouts are supposed to be kept secret, do they?"

Reece raked his fingers through his hair. The more he heard, the more apprehensive he became. "Well, no. But I trust them. I used one of the garages that does insurance work for me."

"So anyone at your office could possibly discover that Maggie has been staying here," Derrick said. "And didn't you say," he went on, "that you had the car towed from her house and delivered here to your house? The towing-service people could—"

"Okay, okay, I see what you mean." Reece felt his worry turn to icy distress. Some lunatic could be out there right now, stalking Maggie, following her with malicious intent.

"Giving Maggie time to sort out her feelings is one thing," Jason said with quiet firmness. "But, Reece, she could be in danger. Grave danger."

It took Reece only two seconds to decide what to do. "Come on, guys. Let's go look through her files and see what we can find."

Maggie was on the hunt. From her preliminary investigation of Anthony Arnor, she had discovered that the sheriff had been spending an inordinate amount of time with the owner of Bayview's only jewelry store, a beautiful and vivacious widow.

Shifting her position, Maggie tried once again to get comfortable on the dirt-packed ground. Unfortunately, the leaf-laden branches of the straggly hedge bushes under which she sat prohibited the sunlight from reaching the grass beneath, so there was little cushioning for her bottom. She regretted having to leave her car up the road a couple of blocks; however, her hiding spot at the side of the yard gave her a terrific view of the house. Of course, the downside was that she was on the widow's private property, which could cause a bit of a problem if she were to be discovered. But since there was really no way to get around it, she decided the best solution to that dilemma was not to get caught.

The pictures she'd snapped of Arnor entering the widow's house would serve as proof for the man's wife. Now all that Maggie needed was documentation that the sheriff had visited his mistress long enough for some hanky-panky to have taken place. Maggie decided she'd wait him out another hour; that should certainly be long enough to convince Betty Arnor of her husband's infidelity.

Once all the evidence had been turned over to the sheriff's wife, Maggie would be free to go home. The thought left her feeling desolate and lonely.

Her days with Jeff had stirred in her an emotion, a love for the child that was almost maternal. She loved his impish grin, his wide-eyed, wondrous way of looking at the world. She was going to miss the boy terribly.

And then there was Reece. He'd been so good to her. So giving. So kind. And he'd adamantly denied wanting anything in return.

However, he *had* benefited from her presence in his home, the logical voice inside her pointed out. He'd had a sitter for his son, a trained counselor who gently questioned the child's attitude toward women. Besides, the voice analyzed, there is no way Reece could be different from any other man you've dealt with—Peter, Buster, Sheriff Arnor... The list of hurtful, cheating, conniving men went on and on. Reece was a man, and although all of them were certain to have their good points, there always came a time when they used the women in their lives.

The thought saddened her. Because there was a part of her—the soft, feminine, emotional side—that wanted more than anything for Reece to be different. A side of her that desperately wanted—

Maggie froze when the outside light of the neighboring house switched on. The side door opened and a small dog scampered out into the fenced yard.

"Hurry up, now, Baby," a gentle, aged voice called. "Go potty so we can go to bed."

The collie made a beeline for the hedge bushes, and

after sniffing at the fence just inches from Maggie's back, the animal growled under its breath.

"It's okay," Maggie crooned in a whispery tone. "I'm harmless, Baby. Really I am." Panic welled up in her. All she needed was for the dog to start barking. Maggie fumbled in her pocket. "Here, girl." She tossed a cheese cracker at the dog. "Now be a good little dog and go away."

After greedily gobbling up the treat, the dog continued to growl.

"Shoo," Maggie ordered.

The collie barked, and Maggie scrambled for another cracker to toss.

"Baby!" the dog's owner yelled sternly. "Quiet! You'll wake the neighbors."

The collie barked again.

"That's it," the elderly lady called. "Come!"

However, Baby continued to protect her turf.

The outside light of the widow's house switched on. Maggie's eyes grew wide, and perspiration beaded across her upper lip. She tossed the dog the last cracker. "Please, go away," she pleaded softly.

Baby's owner took a step out into the night. "Come!" she ordered. "Now!"

The collie finally obeyed, but not before squatting down and relieving herself beside the fence, inches from Maggie's foot.

"Thanks a lot," Maggie grumbled as the dog dashed off.

The air hadn't settled for two seconds before she heard a car traveling down the road. The widow's house sat in a residential neighborhood, so the arrival of the car wasn't so odd; however, the fact that the driver turned off the headlights as it cruised by was suspicious.

Maggie watched the car pass the house very slowly. Then she heard rather than saw it stop. The engine switched off. What the hell was going on? Maggie wondered. Was someone else checking up on Sheriff Arnor? The county police force? Or maybe someone was investigating the widow's exploits....

Before she could ponder everything out, Maggie heard a car door open and shut. Her heart hammered. There were footsteps, first on the sidewalk, then on the grass.

"Psst, Maggie," she heard a husky voice whisper, "where are you?"

Reece? What was he doing here?

"Psssssst." His tone rose just a little. "Maggie."

The idiot was going to ruin everything! She scrambled from her hiding place, but stayed in the shadows as much as possible.

"Here. I'm over here." She kept her voice low, but was unable to quell the frantic quality of it.

Reece trotted up the side of the yard and squatted down beside her.

"What do you think you're doing?" The question spurted from her like air from a punctured tire, fast and furious.

"I need to talk to you," he said. "You've got the wrong—"

"Are you crazy? You're going to get me caught here. I'm working!"

"Wait. Listen to me—"

"How did you find out where to find me?" As soon as the words left her mouth, she knew the answer, and she gasped in outrage. "You ransacked my files!"

The guilty expression on his face told her she'd guessed correctly. She glared. "How could you do such a thing?"

"Who's out there?"

Maggie's gaze whipped toward the door where she saw Sheriff Arnor standing on the step peering out into the darkness.

"Darn it, Reece! Now look what you've done. What the heck are we going to tell him? How are we ever going to explain…?" She let the question die on her lips as Arnor crossed the yard.

"Do you people realize this is private property?"

The sheriff's distinguished face didn't show any anger, and that surprised Maggie. Having thoroughly dug into his background, she knew he'd turn sixty on his next birthday. He'd acted as the county sheriff for more than twenty years. Maggie expected him to show a little emotion since he was involved in a scandal that just might jeopardize all he'd worked for.

"Yes, sir," she said, lifting her chin. "We do."

Arnor's gaze darted to the camera that hung from a wide black strap around her neck. Lord, she was going to have to come up with a whopper of a lie to get them out of this one.

"Who are you?" the man repeated. "And who are your friends?"

Maggie's brows shot heavenward. "Friends?"

"Yeah," Arnor said. "You *are* with the two guys who're standing on the corner there, right?" With a jerk of his head, he indicated the sidewalk that ran along the front of the property.

This time, Reece answered. "Yes, sir. They're with us."

Maggie shifted her surprised expression toward Reece.

His shrug was accompanied with a sheepish look. "It's Derrick and Jason."

"What is going on, Reece?" she asked. "Why are they here?"

Arnor looked at Reece. "I'd like to know, too." Then he turned his sharp eyes on Maggie. "But I have a good idea of who you are. You're a reporter, aren't you? And you're aiming to tell the whole county about my secret, huh?"

His demeanor wasn't at all what she thought it should be. She expected anger, resentment, misplaced blame; instead, he was evincing a complacency that could almost be described as amiable. It was almost as if he expected her to be here, expected to be caught, and that he felt that was no big deal.

The sheriff's behavior ruffled her ire. "I'm not a reporter," she snapped. "But maybe I'll go call one, because I'd just love it if the county discovered that you're a liar and a cheat!"

"What?" Arnor looked as if she'd sucker punched him in the jaw.

"Come on, Maggie," Reece said, taking her by the arm. "Let's just go."

"No—" she jerked herself from his grasp "—I think I'd like to tell the sheriff here just what I think of him and his kind."

Anthony Arnor's face was the epitome of confusion and innocence. Oh, she thought, he had his act down pat. "Don't you stand there and look at me like you have no idea what I'm talking about. You're as guilty as sin and you know it."

Darting a glance at Reece, the sheriff asked, "What in blue blazes is she talking about? Guilty of what?"

Reece pressed his lips together, raised his hands and shook his head. Words obviously failed him.

Arnor's innocent act irritated her. Why couldn't the man just be honest?

Then Maggie saw Reese's friends, Derrick and Jason,

approaching them. What were they doing here? The question glinted through her mind like the flash of her camera.

Men. They were all around her, and she couldn't seem to figure out even one of them. Suddenly, her breath left her in a sigh. Her shoulders sagged. She felt bone weary. Tired of trying to understand the opposite sex. Tired of feeling disappointed and angry when she discovered men like Anthony Arnor two-timing their wives. Tired of the confusion that roiled inside her each and every time she thought of Reece and how wonderful he made her feel.

She just wanted to go home. She just wanted to slide into bed and hide her head under the covers so she didn't have to deal with any of this anymore.

"She knows," Maggie told Armor, her voice sounding jaded and overly fatigued. "Your wife knows."

"Maggie," Reece warned softly.

Something unnameable glimmered in Arnor's aged eyes. "Betty knows about the necklace? But I was so careful to keep it a secret."

Necklace? What was he talking about?

"I don't know anything about a necklace," she said, plowing ahead. "And as far as I know, neither does Betty. But she *does* know about your mistress."

"Maggie." Reece's voice was sterner this time.

By this time, Reece's two friends had joined them on the lawn, but Maggie was too preoccupied with the sheriff to give them much notice.

"Dear Lord," Arnor exclaimed. "My Betty thinks I'm...I'm stepping out on her?"

"She doesn't *think*," Maggie asserted. "She *knows*."

The man was intelligent enough to put the pieces together quickly. "You're not a reporter, are you?" He hesitated a moment. "You're a PI." His eyes went wide. "My Betty hired a PI?"

Maggie steeled herself for his onslaught of anger. She was happy that Reece was here with her. The thought struck her like a jolt of lightning, and she quickly tried to reason it out. Yes, she admitted that Reece's being here lent her some security. Not that she needed his protection; it was just that she was happy to have his presence. Frustrated with trying to figure it out, she shoved the idea from her brain.

Focusing her mind on the matter at hand, Maggie confirmed, "Betty hired a PI. And she knows that you've been spending your time with a woman by the name of Juliet Dean of Dean's Jewelry."

The Sheriff grew quiet a moment, and that puzzled Maggie. Where was the yelling, the anger, the blaming of others? Why wasn't Anthony Arnor reacting like any other normal, red-blooded male who had been caught with his hand in the cookie jar?

"Oh, my—" Arnor seemed to be speaking to himself, so soft were his words "—poor Betty must be feeling awful if she thinks I've been unfaithful. I hate the idea that my secret has given her even a minute of distress."

He lifted an imploring gaze first to Reece, then to Maggie. "I'm not cheating on my wife. I love Betty with all my heart. And I wouldn't do a thing to hurt her. Not a thing."

His face, his eyes, his words, all seemed honest and open. Nothing at all like the glinty-eyed lies and hollow-sounding excuses she was used to hearing. The irritation drained out of her, and was replaced by calm bewilderment. Could Arnor be telling the truth? she wondered. Well, if he was, there were questions that needed to be answered.

"What are you doing here, Sheriff? Why are you with Juliet Dean, all alone, in the middle of the night?"

He stuffed his hands into the pockets of his trousers. "I've been working on a surprise. A necklace. An emerald-and-diamond necklace specially designed for my Betty." A ghost of a smile passed his lips. "You see, our fortieth wedding anniversary is coming up. And I've spent weeks and weeks going over jewelry designs with Juliet. We meet at her house, at night, 'cause that's the only way I could figure to keep it a secret."

Maggie's mouth went dry as attic dust. She'd been so certain that Sheriff Arnor was cheating on his wife. She'd been so sure he was just like all the other men she'd investigated. All the other men she'd caught in one illicit act or another.

"I need to go call my wife," Arnor said. "I've got to set her straight. To heck with the surprise."

However, Maggie had become so caught up in the jumbled thoughts tumbling around in her brain that the man's voice sounded far-off and hazy. She became vaguely aware of Arnor engaging Reece's friends in conversation.

"Maggie."

Reece's gentle tone entered the fog floating around in her head.

"Are you okay?"

She didn't answer him, only studied his handsome face. He had told her he wasn't like Peter. He had tried to explain that his reasons for offering her his help were free and clear of any ulterior motives. Yet she had refused to believe him.

Could it be that her domestic-affairs duties as a cop and then her experiences as a PI had warped her idea of what men represented? Had her experiences with so many dark and abusive personalities twisted her view of men in general?

"Maggie…"

Reece's whispery voice once again probed the haze of her thoughts.

"Talk to me."

But she needed time alone. Time to sort this all out. Time to clear her mind, and to ponder this mayhem she was going through. She shook her head.

"Not right now," she told him, her tone sounding distant to her own ears. She turned and took a step away from the men. "I'll see you at home."

"Wait, Maggie." Reece stopped her with a hand on her shoulder. "You shouldn't be alone."

Maggie blinked, and his face actually came into focus. She reached up and pressed her palm against his jaw. "I want to talk to you, Reece. And I will. I just need to be alone for a few minutes. I'll see you back at your house."

The night was still, the street quiet, as she walked toward her car. But then, the world could have fallen around her ears for all the notice she took.

Sheriff Arnor had every reason to blast Maggie. She'd been on private property. She'd taken pictures of his entering the widow's house—pictures she planned to hand over to his wife. She'd accused him of cheating on Betty. Yes, the man certainly had enough reasons to vent his anger on her.

However, he'd remained calm and collected as he tried to discover her motives for being on Juliet Dean's property. And when Maggie's irritation had prompted her to taunt the man, when she'd accused him of having a mistress, Arnor's first thought had been for his wife. He'd expressed his distress that he'd caused her even a moment of worry. The man must be a wonderful husband.

When she put this information together with her agonizing confusion regarding Reece, his character and his motives, Maggie realized she had some serious rethinking to do. Her generalizations where men were concerned had nearly cost her everything. And her broad and sweeping negative opinions about men were just as bad as, if not worse than, young Jeff's chauvinistic attitude toward women. At least Jeff had his youth as an excuse. She was supposed to be an intelligent, free-thinking woman. How could she have let herself become trapped by such ideas? And how was she ever going to explain herself to Reece? And since she'd once again put him off, would he even be interested in listening?

The sound of footsteps on the sidewalk behind her caught her attention, and she stopped, intending to turn around. Before she could, hands caught her up like steel bands, hot fingers pressing against her mouth. Panic rushed through her body, tensing her muscles.

"There you are," a raspy voice whispered into her ear. "I've been watching for you."

The man's lips were so close that his words seemed to be shouted. Disjointed, fractured thoughts thundered through her head. Her gun. Tucked in her purse. Out of reach. Break away. Escape. Run.

"I had such a grand time playing with your mind. Scaring you witless. But then you left. I couldn't find you," he said, his spittle flecking her ear and neck. "You really pissed me off. But now I've got you."

His chuckle was cocky, and it seemed to boom into Maggie's eardrum so loudly that she flinched. That voice sounded familiar.

"I wasn't going to hurt you. Just mess with your head to teach you a lesson. But now she's dead," he went on. "And they arrested Russell, and it's all your fault. You're going to pay, you bitch."

Adrenaline pumped into her body, hot and frantic. She was in trouble. Deep trouble. She blinked, her mind whirling. Reece. His name echoed in her mind like a saving grace. Reece would help her. He would be there for her. Just like always.

Ripping and clawing at the fingers clamped against her lips, Maggie was only able to pull them away a fraction. But it was enough.

Her scream slashed the black silence of the night.

The next few minutes passed in what seemed like slow motion. She fought the man who held her captive. Heard the shouts of Reece, his friends and the sheriff.

"Joey!"

The man froze, then viciously twisted both himself and her around to face the direction from which the other men came.

Reece had called the man's name, Maggie realized. Joey, he'd said. Then it dawned on her. Joey worked in Reece's office. The adjuster who had continuously rejected her claims.

"It's *her* fault, Reece," Joey shouted.

His voice took on a plaintive quality, and Maggie felt a hot tear scald her neck.

"Debbie is dead because of *her*. And now Russell's in jail."

"No, Joey." Reece inched closer. "Your sister-in-law is dead because your brother beat her into a coma. Your brother killed Debbie, Joey. Let Maggie go. All she did was gather information on Russell. Information that Debbie paid for. It was a job for Maggie. That's all."

Police sirens sounded in the distance, and Maggie felt the man's head jerk upright. Joey shoved her forward, hard, and then took off into the night.

Maggie crashed against her parked car, broken glass raining around her. She lay there, too stunned to even lift herself from where she had fallen in the gutter.

"Are you okay?"

Reece's gentle hands pulled her up and pressed her against his chest.

"God, please say you're all right, Maggie."

"I'm okay," she said. "Where is he? Where's Joey?"

"They're after him." He smoothed his hand over her hair. "Jason, Derrick and the sheriff. Joey hasn't got a chance." Tucking his curled fingers under her chin, he lifted her face until their gazes met. "Let me look at you. You're sure you're okay? There's glass. The side mirror is broken. Are you bleeding?"

The concern in his voice, in his eyes, melted her heart. She'd suffered so much confusion about this man; however, the kindness and caring he poured on her was like a ray of sunshine burning up the haze. Her mind was suddenly clear, her thoughts like crystal.

"I don't think I'm bleeding," she told him softly. She looked down. "Oh, no," she groaned. "It's my camera. The lens is smashed to pieces."

"It's okay," he said. "As long as you're not hurt." He pressed a velvet kiss on her temple.

"Reece, it was Joey. He was the one breaking into my house."

He nodded. "When I read your files, I saw Joey's brother listed there."

"It was a pitifully small file. I hadn't worked for Debbie long before her husband put on a little-good-boy act. Debbie fell for it. She wanted to save her marriage. I told her not to tell him she'd hired me." A cloud of sadness descended on her as she remembered. "But women often bare their souls in some misguided effort to fix what they think is wrong in their relationships." She looked up at Reece. "Russell pounded Debbie so badly, he put her into the hospital only days after she'd hired me. Russell killed Debbie. He killed her.''

Two police cars pulled up to the curb. Jason and the sheriff loaded a subdued Joey into a cruiser. Maggie watched the police officers talk with Jason and Derrick. She wanted to cry. The nightmare was over. A tear trickled slowly down her face. Reece smoothed the pad of his thumb across her cheek, capturing the teardrop.

"Thank you for being here," she whispered. "I have so much to tell you. So much to say. I've been wrong. About you. About a lot of things."

His dark eyes turned to burnished silk. "I love you, Maggie."

The tears that flowed had nothing whatsoever to do with Joey and the nightmare she'd been living.

"And I love you." She searched his gaze. "I almost lost you because I was too afraid to trust you. Why didn't I realize that I could trust you with my life—?"

"Hush," he said. And then he kissed her softly, gently. "I had the same problem."

"But at least you admitted it. At least you wanted to change for Jeff."

"And for you."

Her heart swelled with a love so sweet, it was painful.

The sheriff approached them. "You okay?" he asked Maggie.

She nodded.

Arnor pointed at Jason, who stood back a couple of steps. "This guy did a fantastic job of catching that jerk."

Maggie smiled her thanks at Jason.

"We'll need a statement," he went on, "but that can wait until tomorrow when you're feeling better."

She nodded, and the small group of men began to walk away, but not before she heard Arnor say to Jason,

"You've got a great reputation on the town force. You know, I'm going to be retiring in a few years. You ought to think about taking the job...."

She looked up at Reece. "It really is all over, isn't it?"

"It sure is."

"And you were there for me through the whole mess."

He grinned. "I sure was."

"And you really weren't looking for anything in return." She studied him a moment. "I love you so much."

Reece's lips were warm, heavenly, against hers. She pressed her palm against his chest, and he looked at her questioningly.

She bit her bottom lip a moment before she spoke. "Do you think my camera will be covered by my insurance?"

He rolled his eyes in mock frustration. Then he laughed outright. "I'll buy you a new camera," he told her. Then his voice lowered to a sexy octave as he added, "As a wedding gift."

Epilogue

Maggie stood on the white sandy beach of Key Largo, Florida, and knew she was in paradise. Palm trees, warm sunshine, crashing waves, gentle breezes and the faint call of a sea gull.

She had never thought she would ever feel this happy, this content. She had just pledged to love, honor and cherish Reece for the rest of her days, and he had done the same to her. And now she listened with quiet joy as the minister orchestrated the vows between her new friends Jason Devlin and Katie Wellingford. The old married couple of the group, Derrick and Anna Cheney, had come along on the trip to act as best man and matron of honor for both couples.

The double-wedding ceremony had been the brainstorm of the men of the group. Jason had been trying to get Katie to agree to a marriage date for months, but Katie's parents, Senator and Mrs. Wellingford, had continued to drive poor Katie half-crazy with their insistence on a large wedding.

Finally, Derrick, Jason and Reece had decided that the three couples should take their brand-new sailboat, the *Club II*, on her maiden voyage, along the Intracoastal Waterway to the southern tip of Florida, where Jason and Reece could wed their brides. It would be the perfect solution for them all. So, having found sitters for all the children, they set off on their romantic adventure.

They had intended on having the ceremonies performed in Key West, Florida's southernmost point; however, Reece simply couldn't wait, and he'd stated that he'd wage mutiny if the group didn't agree to dock in Key Largo so Maggie could become his wife.

She smiled now just thinking about his impatience. She loved the man to distraction, and she knew that his love for her was deep, and real, and intimate. A love that would last a lifetime.

"I now pronounce you—" the minister suffered a moment of confusion over what words to speak as he gazed at the four of them, then he shrugged and smiled "—husbands and wives. You may kiss your brides."

Reece enfolded her in his arms. He tasted of sea salt and warm sunshine. She parted her lips for him, entwining her fingers in his thick black hair.

He pulled back and gazed at her, love shining in his deep brown eyes. "So," he whispered softly so only she could hear, "how does it feel to finally be Mrs. Newton?"

She smiled at him warmly. "It feels wonderful, Mr. Newton."

"Congratulations!"

Maggie turned to see Anna, Derrick's soft-spoken wife. A smile lit her beautiful, serene face, her colorful scarf and matching gauzy skirt gently flapping in the tropical breeze.

"Thanks," Maggie said.

Anna was a schoolteacher, a woman who adored children, a woman who, unfortunately, couldn't have children of her own. However, all along the trip south, she had talked of raising "oodles" of boys and girls, as many as she and Derrick could adopt. Maggie was certain her new friend would do just that.

Derrick wished her well and kissed her on the cheek, then he shook Reece's hand. He did the same to Katie and Jason.

As soon as she saw that Katie was free, Maggie went to her. "Well," she told Katie, "we did it. We took the giant step."

Katie smiled and hugged her. "We sure did."

Maggie had been a little frightened of Katie at first. When Reece had told Maggie that Katie was a debutante of sorts, the daughter of a United States senator, Maggie had expected the woman to be cool and distant in character. But she'd been pleasantly surprised to find that Katie was warm and very down-to-earth.

"Congratulations, lady."

Smiling up at Jason for a moment, Maggie then gave him a quick hug. "Same to you," she said.

Jason was a special man. He had spent lots of time with her and Reece during the terrible ordeal of Joey's trial. Together, they had learned how Joey and his brother, Russell, had suffered terrible physical abuse at the hands of their parents; however, the judge had proclaimed that that fact didn't make the men any less responsible for their actions. Russell would remain in prison for the rest of his life. Joey, on the other hand, had a chance to fare better—if he took advantage of the mandatory counseling that went along with his jail term. Maggie was relieved that the ordeal was finally over.

A loud pop startled her.

"Champàgne, anyone?" Derrick called.

"Ooh, my favorite," Anna said.

Katie lifted her glass toward the bottle with a laugh. "Mine, too."

Maggie hurried forward. "Don't forget me."

Reece heaved a sigh. "Did anyone think to bring some beer?"

"Yeah," Jason chimed in, "I'd like a cold one myself about now."

Derrick handed them both glasses of champagne. "We will not toast your weddings with beer. Drink this and like it."

Both men gave in with good-natured shrugs and took the wine.

"Now," Derrick said, "the Single Daddy Club is *definitely* no more. The question is, do we dissolve the club altogether—" there was a collective gasp all around that had Derrick grinning "—or do we simply rename the club."

"Rename the club!"

"Hear, hear!"

They stood there a moment, everyone holding on to their wineglasses waiting for a suggestion.

"Well," Maggie shyly said, "how about just…The Club?"

A cheer burst from them, and they clapped.

"To The Club!" Reece lifted his glass, and everyone followed his lead. There was the sound of several tings as crystal met crystal, and then they all enjoyed a sip of pale, sparkling champagne.

Reece pulled Maggie to him, and she flattened her palm against his broad chest.

"I can't believe you're all mine," he whispered seductively.

"Well, believe it, mister." She grinned. "And you're all mine."

He pressed his lips close to her ear. "I have a gift waiting for you back at the boat."

Sentiment glittered in her gaze. She suspected his gift was the new camera he'd promised her.

"How about a nice long walk on the beach?" he suggested. "Just the two of us."

"I'd love it."

He wrapped his arm securely around her waist, as though he was afraid someone might take her away from him. She loved this protective instinct of his. It made her feel warm. It made her feel loved. And it was a feeling she wanted to savor forever.

As they walked on the pure, white sand toward the sapphire water, they heard Jason complain, "Didn't somebody think to toss a beer into that wicker basket? I wanna beer!"

Reece and Maggie shared a long and loving laugh, and she knew it was only the first of many.

* * * * *

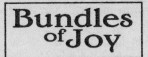

Take 4 bestselling love stories FREE

Plus get a FREE surprise gift!

Special Limited-time Offer

Mail to Silhouette Reader Service™

3010 Walden Avenue
P.O. Box 1867
Buffalo, N.Y. 14240-1867

YES! Please send me 4 free Silhouette Romance™ novels and my free surprise gift. Then send me 6 brand-new novels every month, which I will receive months before they appear in bookstores. Bill me at the low price of $2.67 each plus 25¢ delivery and applicable sales tax, if any.* That's the complete price and a savings of over 10% off the cover prices—quite a bargain! I understand that accepting the books and gift places me under no obligation ever to buy any books. I can always return a shipment and cancel at any time. Even if I never buy another book from Silhouette, the 4 free books and the surprise gift are mine to keep forever.

215 BPA A3UT

Name	(PLEASE PRINT)	
Address	Apt. No.	
City	State	Zip

This offer is limited to one order per household and not valid to present Silhouette Romance™ subscribers. *Terms and prices are subject to change without notice. Sales tax applicable in N.Y.

USROM-696   ©1990 Harlequin Enterprises Limited

And the Winner Is...
You!

...when you pick up these great titles
from our new promotion at your
favorite retail outlet this June!

Diana Palmer
The Case of the Mesmerizing Boss

Betty Neels
The Convenient Wife

Annette Broadrick
Irresistible

Emma Darcy
A Wedding to Remember

Rachel Lee
Lost Warriors

Marie Ferrarella
Father Goose

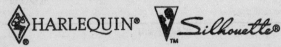

As seen on TV!
Free Gift Offer

With a Free Gift proof-of-purchase from any Silhouette® book,
you can receive a beautiful cubic zirconia pendant.

This gorgeous marquise-shaped stone is a genuine cubic
zirconia—accented by an 18" gold tone necklace.

(Approximate retail value $19.95)

Send for yours today…
compliments of ▼ *Silhouette*®
™

To receive your free gift, a cubic zirconia pendant, send us one original proof-of-
purchase, photocopies not accepted, from the back of any Silhouette Romance™,
Silhouette Desire®, Silhouette Special Edition®, Silhouette Intimate Moments®
or Silhouette Yours Truly™ title available in February, March and April at your favorite
retail outlet, together with the Free Gift Certificate, plus a check or money order for
$1.65 u.s./$2.15 can. (do not send cash) to cover postage and handling, payable
to Silhouette Free Gift Offer. We will send you the specified gift. Allow 6 to 8 weeks for
delivery. Offer good until April 30, 1997 or while quantities last. Offer valid in the
U.S. and Canada only.

Free Gift Certificate

Name: _____

Address: _____

City: _____ State/Province: _____ Zip/Postal Code: _____

Mail this certificate, one proof-of-purchase and a check or money order for postage
and handling to: SILHOUETTE FREE GIFT OFFER 1997. In the U.S.: 3010 Walden
Avenue, P.O. Box 9077, Buffalo NY 14269-9077. In Canada: P.O. Box 613, Fort Erie,
Ontario L2Z 5X3.

FREE GIFT OFFER   084-KFD
ONE PROOF-OF-PURCHASE
To collect your fabulous FREE GIFT, a cubic zirconia pendant, you must include this
original proof-of-purchase for each gift with the properly completed Free Gift Certificate.

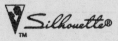